Our Man Weston

Gordon Korman

Our Man Weston

Gordon Korman

Cover by Susan Hall

Scholastic-TAB Publications Ltd.,
123 Newkirk Road, Richmond Hill, Ontario, Canada

ISBN 0-590-71123-7

Published by Scholastic-TAB Publications Ltd., 123 Newkirk Road, Richmond Hill, Ontario, Canada L4C 3G5

1st printing 1982   Printed in Canada.

For Igor Kovalik, with whom I share a room and a stack of neuroses high enough to obscure the Manhattan Smog.

THE UNCERTAINTY PRINCIPLE

The PORTRAITS COLLECTION ™

Beverly Sommers

FAWCETT GIRLS ONLY • NEW YORK

A Fawcett Girls Only Book
Published by Ballantine Books
Copyright © 1990 by Daniel Weiss Associates, Inc.

The PORTRAITS COLLECTION is a trademark owned by Daniel Weiss Associates, Inc.

Library of Congress Catalog Card Number: 90-93136

ISBN 0-449-14608-1

Manufactured in the United States of America

First Edition: October 1990

1

I WAS LYING ON MY BED TELLING MY BEST FRIEND MY latest theory regarding earthquakes. She had looked marginally interested when I started out, but now she was trying to stifle a yawn. I ignored her and shifted my eyes to the far wall.

My bedroom walls, which were cluttered with posters of rock stars my junior year, plastered with sports figures my sophomore year, and papered with pink cabbage roses (my mother's choice) when I was a freshman, were painted a pristine white for my senior year, and absolutely blank. I felt that they mirrored my life, which was also a total blank, along with being boring, boring, boring. . . .

If I had been a poet, I would have taken up a pen and poured out my sense of frustration and futility in metered verse. If I'd been an artist, I would have painted minimalist pictures depicting nothingness. If I had been a rock singer, I would have switched to the blues. Since I lacked artistic talent of any kind, I bitched to Jennifer instead.

I noted that Jennifer was dressed all in black: black tank top, black shorts, even black running shoes. Along with her black hair, she made a nice contrast against my white walls. Jennifer had a way of tossing her head back so that her hair swung away from her face like wings. This, combined with her delicate, birdlike movements, made her seem at times about to take flight. Now the black seemed to ground her, the dense color rooting her more firmly to the earth.

I had a feeling that the black was her way of expressing mourning over her break-up with Steve. A little dramatic for my taste, but Jennifer was always one to seek out the potential drama in any situation.

I finished telling Jennifer my latest theory, which was that the big earthquake would be of such gigantic proportions that it would throw everyone in California back in time.

Jennifer sighed, and then she said, "You know something, Kathy? You're really getting weird."

"Why? Because I want to talk about something besides Steve?"

A tear exited Jennifer's left eye and started rolling down her face. "Well, I'm depressed enough without hearing about earthquakes," she said. "Steve dumping me like this could affect the rest of my life."

I rolled my eyes toward the ceiling. "That's exactly what you said when your mother wouldn't let you have a motorcycle."

I saw the corners of her mouth twitch. "That was different."

"You thought it was the end of the world."

She was starting to smile now. "Okay, so I exaggerate sometimes."

"Most of the time."

"Well, okay, but not all of the time."

"I'm glad to see you still have your sense of humor, Jen."

"Not about Steve, I don't."

"Go on, talk about it if you want to." After all, she always listened to me when I complained about something. And boys were very good material to complain about.

"I'm tired of talking about it," she said.

"I mean it. I don't mind listening."

"I don't feel like talking about Steve. He can go to hell for all I care. He can be a real jerk sometimes, you know?"

I decided to take her at her word that she didn't want to talk about Steve, and I said, "The thing about earthquakes is, there's no warning."

"There wasn't any warning with Steve, either," she said, obviously not ready to change the subject. "Wham! It was over, just like that."

"That doesn't make sense," I told her. "There must have been *some* reason."

"Not any good reason."

"Something like that doesn't just come out of nowhere."

"With Steve it did," she argued. "Steve seems to be coming out of nowhere half the time, anyway."

"Good, keep criticizing him," I said. "Pretty soon you'll wonder why you ever went out with him in the first place."

I got off the bed and went over to my dresser. I brushed my hair back and put a ponytail holder around it, then began to braid it. I thought I felt a slight movement beneath my feet.

I turned to Jennifer. "Did you feel that?"

"Feel what?"

"Did you feel the floor move?"

"You're imagining it, Kathy."

"You didn't feel it?"

"Sometimes I think you're willing an earthquake to happen."

"Maybe I am," I said. Maybe wanting something to change in my life was enough to do it. Maybe, by concentrating really hard, I could change the world.

"Don't even talk like that," said Jennifer. She came over to the mirror and stood beside me. Our reflections were like lightness and dark.

"You want to go to the mall?" Jennifer asked, sounding hopeful. Sometimes I got the idea that going to the mall was Jennifer's reason for living.

"I'll be happy if I never have to see that mall again," I said. All summer I'd been working as a salesperson at a trendy clothing store in Huntington Mall, and yesterday was my last day. It wasn't a bad job, it's just that I very quickly became very tired of clothes, which I've never had Jennifer's passion for.

"You could spend some of the money you made," Jennifer said.

"I don't want to spend it."

"What are you saving it for?"

"I don't know," I said, not wanting to explain.

What was I supposed to say, that it was my escape money? If I told her that, she'd *really* think I was weird. Anyway, it was nice to have a few hundred dollars tucked away, just in case. Like in case I didn't feel like going to college next year, or in case I decided I didn't want to get married, or in case an earthquake hit and left me homeless.

"We could go to a movie," Jennifer suggested.

"We're going tonight," I reminded her. "I don't feel like sitting through two movies in one day."

"We could watch some videos."

"It's too nice to sit inside all day."

"How about the beach?" she asked, knowing I was the one who usually wanted to go to the beach.

I gave a halfhearted nod, but even the idea of swimming didn't appeal to me.

There are no words to describe how bored I was with malls and movies and beaches. Everything was the same, nothing ever changed. The only thing I had to look forward to was school starting in two days, and even an earthquake sounded better than that.

I saw a vision, golden and free, sailing in toward shore on a breaking wave. I held my breath, dazzled for a moment, and then the vision turned into my brother Kevin.

"He's really gotten good, you know that?" said Jennifer, who was also watching him.

"He should be, that's all he does," I said. But I was secretly jealous. I wished I had something that moved me the way surfing moved Kevin. All it took to make him supremely happy was a wave, and there was no shortage of waves in Huntington Beach.

I wondered what would make me supremely happy.

"Do you think I'm doing the right thing? You don't think it's too soon?" Jennifer asked me for the eleventh time in one hour.

"Jennifer, it's only a date. And you're going with us, so what are you worried about?"

"I don't know. I guess I wish I were more excited about it. Do you remember when we used to get excited about dates?"

"Barely."

"Well, you and Eddie, you're practically like a married couple. But a first date you ought to get excited about, don't you think?"

What had happened to all that excitement? When had the excitement turned into complacency? "Alan's probably excited enough for both of you," I said.

"Don't even say that." She rolled over on her back and reached for the suntan oil. "I don't think I'm going to like being a senior. Do you realize that all the new boys in school are going to be fourteen years old?"

"They were last year, too."

"But last year we had the seniors to flirt with."

"You were going with Steve last year."

"Well, if I hadn't been. I can't wait for next year."

"It's not going to be that different," I said, speaking aloud my secret fear.

Contents

1

There is no crime here!

Tom Weston looked out the train window at the countryside racing by. He was reclining contentedly in his seat, chewing on a tuna sandwich.

"Ah, Sidney, we've got it made," he said to his twin brother who sat beside him. "After years of cutting lawns and washing cars we've finally latched onto the best summer jobs anyone could want. Eight whole weeks at a beautiful resort hotel—swimming, tennis, sunshine—a paid vacation."

"And we'll meet a lot of interesting people," Sidney added.

Tom glanced sharply at his brother, then smiled. "Of course they'll want us to do a little work for our salaries, but that's okay. How hard can it be cleaning the occasional ashtray, lugging a few suitcases and loading dishwashers?"

"No problem," agreed Sidney with an identical smile. "And we'll have lots of spare time to devote to our own interests."

1

Tom's serenity faded slightly. "Then again, we *will* have to keep busy. Don't forget our boss, that Mr. Parson. If he isn't the meanest man in the world, he's close. Remember our interview? He seemed to be bawling us out in advance for things we *might* do."

"I'm kind of worried about him myself," admitted Sidney. "I like to be given a free hand when I'm on my own time. Parson sounded as if he might ride herd on us even when we're off duty."

Tom frowned. "What *do* you plan to do when you're off duty?"

Sidney shrugged. "Oh, you know. Things. Whatever comes up."

"How could anything possibly 'come up'?" his brother asked tersely. "The Pine Grove Resort Hotel is a vacation paradise. There are no plots, no crimes, no embezzlements, no murders, no spies, no corrupt officials, no great wrongs that need righting. *No one* there will be doing anything illegal. There will be no reason for you to investigate anything!"

Sidney chewed thoughtfully on his sandwich. "Did you know that there's a military air base adjoining the hotel property?"

"A military air base?" Tom was becoming alarmed. "How could you know about that?"

"I enlarged the photograph on the hotel brochure," Sidney explained casually. "At magnification nine, there it was. I'll bet they've got lots of pretty big stuff over there," he added. "Maybe even Norad secrets."

2

"Sidney, if it's so top secret they certainly don't want *you* to know about it. Now come back down to earth."

"But it's important—and it's interesting," said Sidney. "You're never interested in anything."

"Maybe if you weren't so nosy about absolutely *everything* our family wouldn't always be in such disgrace."

"I've never disgraced anybody."

"Oh, really? How about all those investigations of yours? They're pretty disgraceful. And what's more, you're always wrong."

"I'm not wrong. I base my conclusions on observation, evidence and previously established fact."

"Oh, sure!" exclaimed Tom. "What was the evidence when you cornered the jewel smuggler and it turned out to be Mom?"

"That was a mistake," muttered Sidney.

"And what about the mysterious shady character in our back yard? You dropped our best lace tablecloth over his head, tied him up with the clothesline, locked him in the tool shed and told the police you'd captured Public Enemy Number One. Then we found out he was from the gas company and all he was trying to do was read the meter! But that was nothing. How about the time you placed all those nuns under citizen's arrest?"

"Okay," said Sidney in exasperation. "Nobody's perfect. Those were just a few unfortunate incidents. It's all different now."

"You bet it is," said Tom through clenched

teeth. "Now I've got a good summer job, and I'm not going to lose it because my brother thinks he's James Bond and I look like my brother!"

Sidney stood up, a picture of righteous dignity. "I don't have to sit here and take all this. I'm going to change my seat."

"You do that! But I'm warning you, if you do anything to get Mr. Parson mad at us, you're dead!"

Sidney bristled. "Are you threatening me?"

"Yes!"

Sidney grabbed his suitcases from the overhead rack, walked to the front of the car and sat down in a vacant seat. Stiffly, he produced a copy of *Counter-Espionage Weekly* and began to read.

I knew this would happen, Tom raged to himself. Why can't the world look the same to Sidney as it does to everyone else? He's going to do all kinds of stupid things and everyone is going to think *I* did them because we have the same face. No way, Sidney Weston! Not this time!

*   *   *

Tom picked up the tray outside the first door on his side of the corridor and placed it on the large cart. Sidney stood across the hall, looking exactly like Tom in black pants and short red jacket, the hotel's service-boy uniform. He picked up his first tray and examined it intently.

"Two women in this room," he observed. "Lipstick on both cups."

4

Tom, walking to his second doorway, hesitated and turned a warning frown on his brother.

"It doesn't matter who's in the rooms. We just work at this hotel, remember? All we have to do is pick up last night's room-service trays."

Sidney paid no attention. Why could Tom never see the possibilities seething in the world around him? He hefted his second tray. "Hmmm. Big poker game in this room."

"How would you know?" asked Tom suspiciously.

"Observe. Upon close inspection, you will note an imprint in what's left of the onion dip. It looks like a poker chip. After I make a close-up high-resolution photograph, I'll be able to tell definitely whether it is or not."

"I don't care if it is and you don't either!" Tom exploded. "Remember what I said on the train. Just pick up the trays and mind your own business!"

"I'm not doing anything," Sidney defended himself. "I'm just thinking. It's not my fault the guests leave such obvious clues lying around."

"Clues to what?" cried Tom. "So what if a guest wants to play poker? These aren't *clues!* They're dirty dishes! Look, Sidney, we've finally got a good summer job. They didn't hire a detective; they hired a service boy. Don't forget our meeting with Parson—he's already disgusted with us because he can't tell us apart. Now you just stop it!"

"Lay off," said Sidney. "Hey, look at that. The

guy in this room must be rich. Last night he smoked three hand-rolled Havana cigars."

"How would you like to eat those butts? Sidney, you have to stop it!"

"Honestly, Tom, I'm just thinking. How can thinking hurt anything?"

"Look, whenever you start thinking you start jumping to conclusions, and before you know it a major investigation is under way. If that happens here, we're fired!"

"Why don't you just leave me alone?" shouted Sidney. "I can't stand the way you—"

"Is this the way the staff behaves in the middle of the hall at the Pine Grove Resort Hotel?" came a cold voice from behind them.

The twins wheeled. Regarding them reproachfully stood Walter Parson, general manager of the hotel.

"This noisy bickering is absolutely unacceptable. A service boy is like a telephone or an ashtray. He is simply there, silent and useful, until needed. Then he performs his duties efficiently *and quietly*. You are here for the convenience of our guests, but waking them up is *not* one of your duties. Alarm clocks serve that function admirably. Is that clear?"

"Yes, sir," said Tom.

Parson turned to Sidney. "And you, Tom?"

"I'm Sidney, sir."

"I beg your pardon?"

"He's Tom," explained Sidney, pointing to his brother. "I'm Sidney."

Parson stared into space for a moment. Then he said, "I am not accustomed to being contradicted. However, since you are new here I will overlook this little outburst. But see to it that it doesn't happen again. Now, continue with your work—*quietly.*"

Tom cast Sidney a furious glare and returned to the business of picking up trays.

* * *

Sidney Weston lay back on his bed in contentment. He was now completely unpacked, and he had five minutes to spare before Tom, who shared the room, came off duty. All his investigation equipment was safely hidden away where his brother would never find it. It was a good thing he had taken advantage of that fantastic offer in *Home Detective Digest* for a copy of *10,000 Useful Hiding Places for Spies and Novices.* Tom just didn't seem to understand that observing human behaviour and studying the criminal mind were important. One never knew when one might stumble onto a crime or a conspiracy. One had to be prepared. And he, Sidney Weston, was prepared.

There was the sound of a key in the lock, and Tom stepped into the room.

"Hi, Sidney. All unpacked?"

"Yup." Sidney got up off his bed and put on his uniform jacket. "There's just one problem. I forgot some clothes."

7

"Oh, I can help you out there. What do you need?"

"Everything."

"What? You mean you didn't bring *any* clothes?"

Sidney shrugged. "I forgot."

"But, Sidney, you had two huge suitcases. What was in them?"

"Oh—you know—just some stuff."

"What kind of stuff?" Tom persisted.

"Just some things I might need."

"For example?"

"Sorry, I have to go," said Sidney, rushing out the door. "I'm on cleaning duty."

Tom held his head in despair. This meant that his brother had brought two enormous suitcases full of detective equipment. He looked around the room. There was no telling where it might be stashed. Sidney was an expert at concealment. He could hide a jeep in a teapot.

Grimly Tom began to search. There was nothing in the closet, nothing under the beds, nothing in the dresser drawers, nothing on the bathroom shelves—nothing. Oh well, he thought, starting his own unpacking, if I can't find the stuff at least Parson won't stumble onto it if he suddenly decides to inspect our room. It would not be easy to explain Sidney's police lab.

Tom sighed. He was going to have to keep a very close eye on his brother.

* * *

Sidney applied a little more polish to the wood panelling in the hall of one of the guest wings. Around the corner strolled Tom, who was taking a look through the building on his off time.

"Hi, Sidney. Lean into that a bit, eh? I can't see my face in it yet."

"It's clean enough," Sidney decided, moving along. He tapped the wall thoughtfully with his index finger. "No hollow places here."

Tom resisted the temptation to kick the bent form. "So how do you like being a service boy?"

"No excitement so far."

"What kind of excitement could there be?"

As if on cue, the door of Suite 237 burst open and an elderly lady rushed out into the hall. "Oh, somebody call the police!" she shrilled. "My purse! My purse is missing!"

Instantly Sidney was at her side. "Don't worry, Ma'am. Everything is under control." He whipped a notebook and pencil out of his pocket. "Let's have the facts of the case. Name, please?"

"We'd better report this to Mr. Parson," said Tom quickly.

"I'm Miss Fuller. Edna Fuller," said the lady, leading Sidney and a reluctant Tom into her room. "I just got back from lunch and my purse is gone!"

Sidney scribbled elaborate notes on his pad.

"We'd better tell Mr. Parson," Tom repeated.

"Tell me," said Sidney thoughtfully, "did anyone leave your lunch table—perhaps after noticing that you didn't have your purse with you?"

9

"Well," she replied, "there was that nice Mr. Kitzel, but I think he only went to the bathroom."

"Kitzel," Sidney repeated, writing it down and marking it carefully with his own personal note code for 'suspect.'

"Sidney . . . " Tom intoned warningly.

"Has this Mr. Kitzel acted suspiciously before?"

"Well—I've only known him for a few days, but I think he cheats at shuffleboard."

"So, in other words," Sidney concluded, "you would consider him a possibly deceitful person."

"Sidney!" exclaimed Tom, aghast.

"I always thought he was such a nice man," said Miss Fuller sadly.

"Looks can be deceiving," replied Sidney evenly. "Right now the facts point directly towards him."

Tom looked around. "There's a purse on the bureau. Is that it?"

"Quiet, please. There's an investigation going on here. Could you describe this Mr. Kitzel, Miss Fuller?"

"Well, he's about sixty or sixty-five, and he's a little bit overweight and rather bald."

Tom walked over and picked up a white leather handbag from the bureau. "Is this it, Miss Fuller? Is this what you're looking for?"

"Tom, please!" said Sidney sharply, not looking up from his note pad. "I think we have enough information to move in on Mr. Kitzel."

10

"Why, it's my purse! You found my purse! Oh, you *are* clever boys!"

Sidney stared from the purse to Miss Fuller to Tom, and back to the purse again. "Very interesting," he said shakily. Across his notes he scribbled the word *Solved* and underlined it.

"How wonderful of you!" Miss Fuller raved on. "I'm going to commend you to the manager."

"No!" cried Tom. "I mean—you really don't have to do that. It's our pleasure."

"You're so polite. And you're so cute, too. As alike as two peas in a pod."

"Thank you very much," said Sidney.

"Thank *you*," she amended. "And don't you worry. I'll keep an eye on that Mr. Kitzel."

"We really have to go now," said Tom, giving Sidney a meaningful elbow in the ribs.

"Certainly, dear. Goodbye, boys."

Tom grabbed Sidney and pulled him out of the room, closing the door. "Don't you ever try to pull something like that again!" he stormed. "This is a respectable resort. Only decent people come here, for rest and relaxation. *There is no crime here!*"

* * *

Richard Knight watched his tee shot soar down the fairway of the seventh hole of the Pine Grove Resort golf course. It landed not ten metres from the green.

"Great shot, Dick!" exclaimed his partner, Bert Cobber.

Knight winced. "Cobber, we are not pals. We have a business arrangement."

Cobber lined up his tee shot, swung mightily and missed. "Yeah, yeah, mate, I know that. Hey, does it count if you miss the ball?"

"Of course it counts," replied Knight icily. "It also counted when you hit into the water hazard and when you picked your ball out of the sand trap and threw it onto the green. Losing a ball is a two-stroke penalty; cheating is somewhat more serious."

Cobber just laughed. "Hey, you noticed that, did you? You really *are* a good spy."

Though his head did not move appreciably, Richard Knight did a quick but thorough scan of the area around him. There was no one else on the course. Then, "Yes, I am. And I'll thank you not to broadcast it. We are on an important assignment here."

"Yeah, you keep telling me that, mate," Cobber continued loudly, "but what *is* this important assignment anyway? You never talk about it. All I know is that it's got something to do with airplanes and that air base over there, because you hired me as a pilot." He pointed towards the air base nearby.

In one swift motion Knight brought his driver down across Cobber's forearm. "*Don't* point," he said softly. "If you would use that head of yours for anything more than a decorative hatrack, you

would realize that our intentions towards that air base are highly illegal. Were the authorities to find out about our activities, we would undoubtedly spend a good many years in prison. Do not talk about that air base, nor look at it, nor point at it, nor even think about it. Leave everything to me. When the time comes, you will be told all that it is necessary for you to know. Until then, keep to your cover story and act like a perfectly normal guest on vacation."

"You can count on me, mate," said Cobber enthusiastically. "Yes, sir. 'I'm an airline engineer and I service those big jumbo jets.' How's that?"

"Tone it down and it will do. And, Cobber, you do not volunteer that information. You simply use it when you must in order to appear an ordinary person. I sincerely hope you know enough about airplanes to get by in the event of a conversation about your supremely insignificant life."

"Sure. And I really am a good pilot, mate." Stealthily Cobber nudged his ball with his foot. "I can fly anything. When I was a cadet my flying partner was Wings Weinberg! What do you think of that, eh?"

"Fascinating," said Richard Knight. "Now, please temper your enthusiasm until it is time to do otherwise. And for pity's sake, stop kicking your ball along the fairway. Do you think I'm blind?"

2

The Legend

Colonel Douglas Cartwright, commanding officer of Trillium Air Base, stood on the tarmac, his corps of officers assembled behind him and the entire complement of enlisted personnel drawn up in ranks behind them. All wore full dress uniform.

"This is a big day for Trillium Base," Cartwright commented to his security chief, Captain Snider.

Snider smiled. "I know, sir. I'm as excited as a kid about this. Wings Weinberg coming to Trillium! When he tests the Osiris HE2, we're going to see some pretty fancy flying."

"That we are," agreed Cartwright. He pointed towards the horizon. "There's the chopper now."

As the parade was called to attention, a huge military helicopter roared into sight, hovered for an instant and then slowly settled down onto the concrete pad, its giant rotor blades raising a small dust storm at its base. The blades slowed, then stopped. The door was flung wide and out filed

14

twenty-one maintenance workers and aircraft engineers.

A young lieutenant walked smartly up to Colonel Cartwright, saluted and presented a sealed envelope.

Cartwright returned the salute, took the envelope and scanned the twenty-one new faces. "Where is Lieutenant-Colonel Weinberg?" he asked.

There was a stir in the group and all eyes turned to the helicopter. There, framed in the doorway, his ribbons and decorations glittering in the bright sunlight, stood Lieutenant-Colonel John Daniel "Wings" Weinberg. There were murmurs as he began to stride towards the reception party, his gait lithe and confident, his uniform crisp and immaculate. Cartwright suppressed an urge to salute first.

"Lieutenant-Colonel Weinberg reporting for duty, sir." He executed a model salute.

"Welcome aboard, Colonel Weinberg. Glad to have you with us. Captain Snider, dismiss the men."

"*Dis-missed!*" bellowed Snider.

The men broke ranks, but no one left the scene. Instead they clustered in small groups, all staring in open admiration at the legendary Wings Weinberg, the greatest test pilot in the world.

*   *   *

Colonel Cartwright leaned back in his desk chair and smiled at Captain Snider and Wings Weinberg, who were sitting across from him. "The Osiris HE2 is the most advanced aircraft in the world. We at Trillium are honoured that our base was chosen for the testing. And we're not surprised that you were chosen as the test pilot, Colonel Weinberg."

Wings smiled engagingly. "I've barely had a chance to glance through the flight manual," he said, "but from what I've seen, it looks like a remarkable aircraft. It'll be a real challenge, testing this one."

"You have my unbounded admiration, sir," Snider put in, almost blushing at being face to face with his hero. "I was there when you test-flew the Water Moccasin Aquaplane, and when you rocketed straight down into the ocean I figured you'd never come up again. What a test!"

"It was all routine, really," said The Legend airily. "The Osiris is going to be much more difficult."

"This is going to be the greatest test flight in airforce history," announced Colonel Cartwright decisively. "I know it."

"I appreciate your confidence, sir," said Wings smoothly.

"Tell me," said Snider conversationally, "when you're faced with a plane like the Osiris—one nobody's ever flown before—doesn't it make you feel fresh and green? I mean, doesn't it bring you back to your cadet days?"

Wings Weinberg turned pale under his tan, and his blue eyes glazed over. "No," he said faintly. "Not my cadet days."

"Snider, a man who can fly a thing like the Osiris HE2 is hardly a cadet," Cartwright snapped.

"What I meant was—"

"It doesn't matter," Cartwright interrupted. "I'm sure Lieutenant-Colonel Weinberg wants to settle in and start studying the flight manual." The commanding officer buzzed his secretary. "Corporal Hayes, show Colonel Weinberg to his quarters."

*   *   *

Dragging his feet, Tom Weston walked tiredly into his room after his shift. Parson had been on his back all morning. He shrugged off his red jacket and opened the closet door. In the deep red glow of a film-developing safe light Sidney was sitting on a small wooden stool, working with his darkroom mini-lab.

"Sidney, what the—"

"Tom, you shouldn't just fling doors open like that," said his brother reprovingly. "You might have ruined my film. But it's okay this time. It's out of the developer and into the fixing solution."

"Forgive me," said Tom with sarcasm in his voice. "I should have known you'd be developing pictures in the closet. What else?"

"That's all right," said Sidney cheerfully, re-

moving several wet prints from the solution with tweezers. He pinned them up on a section of clothesline strung across the closet, plugged in a small hair dryer and began to dry them. "No harm done."

Tom stared at the photographs. They documented the arrival of a guest from the point where he left his car in the parking lot, through the checking-in process, up to his actual arrival in his room.

"Sidney, you've been snooping again. And for what? What's the sense of having pictures of this man?"

Sidney's mind began to race. His brother was obviously not his ally. Tom, in his anxiety to safeguard their jobs, would try to stop him from investigating this suspicious new guest. And suspicious he was! There was an almost audible click as Sidney's thoughts left the problem of Tom's interference and settled on his quarry.

Mr. Lawrence K. Waghorn had acted very strangely in the parking lot and the lobby—nervous and twitching and always looking over his shoulder. And the instant he'd reached his room he'd received a phone call from someone he'd called "Chief," which made him even more nervous. Then he'd given Sidney a big fat tip to get rid of him. Yes, there was more than a little to make one suspicious of Mr. Lawrence K. Waghorn.

"Sidney!" snapped Tom, uneasy at the all-too-familiar expression on his twin's face. "Are you

18

listening to me? What if someone saw you taking those pictures? We could lose our jobs!"

"Oh, don't worry about that," explained Sidney. "I used my micro-camera ring. Nobody can spot that."

"What micro-camera ring? How did you get a micro-camera ring?"

"I bought it. There was a special offer in *Clue* magazine last month. For sixty dollars I got a micro-camera which fits into a special neck chain, a ring and a belt buckle. A real bargain, eh?"

Tom looked sick. "Sidney, you destroy those pictures this minute! What if someone comes into our room and finds them? How will we explain *that* to Mr. Parson?"

"I'll hide them. No one'll find them. You should read *10,000 Useful Hiding Places for Spies and Novices,* Tom. It really comes in handy."

"Yeah, maybe I should," said Tom disgustedly. "Where is it?"

Sidney blinked innocently. "I hid it." He took the now dry Waghorn pictures and slid them into his breast pocket. "I've got to go. I'm on duty." As he walked out the door he was thinking, as soon as I have some time to myself I'll write a letter to the Ministry of Transportation and get identification on the licence of Waghorn's car.

Tom sat down on his bed and waited for his temper to cool enough for him to think straight. Well, this was it, then. If Sidney wanted war, war was what he'd get. He made a silent vow to undo every misguided Sherlock Holmes deed his

brother tried to do. It would not be easy—Sidney was clever and devious. In order to stop him, Tom would have to be even more clever, even more devious.

* * *

"But, chief," said Lawrence K. Waghorn nervously into his telephone, "I just got here. I haven't started the script yet ... Okay, so it's a rush job. How come it wasn't a rush job for the two years you were considering doing the show? ... No, I do *not* know exactly what I'll be writing. All you told me was that you wanted a spy story taking place at a hotel. I need some time to think about the characters and the plot ... Of course tomorrow is too early. Television scriptwriters are human too, you know! You're making a nervous wreck out of me! ... No, don't check with me tomorrow! Give me some time! I haven't even unpacked my typewriter yet! Goodbye!"

He slammed down the receiver, paced the room for a few seconds, then began rummaging madly through his luggage in search of his tranquillizers.

"Great outline they gave me," he muttered aloud. "*Spy story—hotel.* That's a real help! Nothing to it now. All I have to do is develop the characters and work out the entire plot so that it's new and original. I couldn't go into my father's delicatessen! No, not me! I had to be a television scriptwriter!"

20

To help calm himself down, he began to un-
pack.

*　　*　　*

"Snider, would you please try to contain your
wonder and awe when you're around Colonel
Weinberg," said Colonel Cartwright testily.

Snider flushed. "I'm sorry, sir."

"I mean, I know he's your hero and all, but
you're upsetting the man. Look how embarrassed
he got in my office when you mentioned feeling
like a cadet again."

"Actually, sir, I don't think that was embar-
rassment. I don't know what it was. He looked
almost sick. Maybe he's just tired."

"It doesn't matter," said Cartwright. "Just re-
strain yourself a little. I don't want anything to
interfere with his concentration. We don't want
Norad to say that Trillium Base didn't provide
perfect conditions for the Osiris test."

"Yes, sir. Are you having dinner with Colonel
Weinberg?"

"As a matter of fact, I am," replied the commanding officer. "Why don't you join us? But no
hero worship, right?"

"Yes, sir."

*　　*　　*

"Hello, there," said Edna Fuller at Table 19 of
the busy Pine Grove dining room. "You're Tom
Weston, aren't you?"

"No, Ma'am, I'm Sidney." He began to stack the used dishes onto his large bus-tray.

"Oh, you've come to pick up the dishes. Isn't that nice, *Mr. Kitzel?*" She gestured meaningfully at the elderly gentleman seated beside her, while nodding energetically at Sidney.

Two other guests at the table were having a chat.

"What line of work are you in?"

"I'm in men's wear."

Bert Cobber could not resist jumping into the conversation. "I'm an airline engineer. I service those big jumbo jets."

Richard Knight looked away in sheer disgust.

"That's an interesting job," commented Lawrence Waghorn. He smiled wanly. "A lot quieter and more peaceful than my job. What airline do you work for?"

Cobber's face went completely blank. He had not been prepared for such a question.

Sidney picked up Mr. Kitzel's glass.

"Didn't you mention you worked for Trans-Atlantica Airlines?" asked Knight.

"Yeah!" exclaimed Cobber in great relief. "That's it, Trans-Atlantica!"

"I thought so," said Knight.

Sidney had worked his way around the table to Waghorn's place. With a dexterity that showed years of practice he pulled a piece of waxed paper out of his sleeve, wrapped it around Waghorn's water glass and slipped the glass into his inside jacket pocket. He glanced nonchalantly around

the table. The guests were busy eating, all except Richard Knight who was regarding him with one raised eyebrow.

"Are you planning to have that analyzed?" Knight asked in quiet amusement.

Sidney turned beet-red and retreated hastily to the kitchen.

"You took your time," complained Tom, who was scraping plates and loading the dishwasher. He took Sidney's tray and nested it on top of the one he had just unloaded. "Hey, what's that in your pocket?"

"Oh—nothing." Sidney turned to leave the kitchen.

"Where are you going? You're still on duty, remember?"

"I've got to go to our room for a second."

"Tom Weston, where are you going?" Mr. Parson approached them. "I certainly hope that you two are not bickering again." He stared at Sidney. "What is that ridiculous bulge in your uniform?" he demanded, pulling the wrapped glass out of Sidney's pocket. "What is the meaning of this, Tom? Must we count the silverware after every meal?"

"I'm not Tom, sir. I'm Sidney."

"Don't evade the issue!" stormed Mr. Parson.

"Well, sir," said Sidney, "uh—there wasn't any room on the tray so I put that glass in my pocket."

"And the waxed paper?" prompted the manager.

"I didn't want to damage the glass. I'm very conscientious about hotel property."

"So I see," commented Mr. Parson icily. He glared at the twins distastefully, removed the paper from the glass and handed it to Tom, who placed it in the dishwasher. "Just remember, I'm watching you—both of you." He walked away stiffly.

"Get back to work!" hissed Tom.

*   *   *

Lawrence Waghorn wrenched the sheet of paper from his typewriter, crumpled it into a ball and hurled it viciously across the room, sending angry words resounding after it.

"How can I write a TV show when I don't have a plot? What am I going to write about? What the devil am I going to write about?"

He got up and began pacing around the room. He switched on the TV set, then switched it off again. In his mind he made a list of all the professions he could have gone into instead of script-writing, and lamented each and every one of them.

"I could have been a stockbroker," he muttered aloud, "but I had to have creative freedom! And what did I get? *Spy story—hotel!*"

Desperately he strode over to the window and looked out. It was almost dark. There were still a few guests in the pool, but the golf course was deserted. What kind of spying could there be in a place like this? People came here for vacations. Espionage! It was all ridiculous!

24

Frustrated, he walked over to the typewriter and sat down. *Spy story—hotel: story involving espionage taking place at hotel,* he typed, and then went completely blank. In disgust he ripped the paper out of the machine, crumpled it up and threw it on the floor. Then he picked it up and examined it again. With a snort of rage he tossed it across the room onto his room-service tray where it came to rest in a pool of spilled coffee.

*   *   *

"I'm not drunk, mate. I'm perfectly in control of myself," exclaimed Bert Cobber indignantly.

"You are very drunk, Cobber," said Richard Knight icily. "You are drawing attention to yourself. If you touch another drop while we are on this assignment, I shall certainly break your fingers."

"But, Dick," protested Cobber, "you told me to act like I was on vacation. What's a vacation without a few drinks?"

"Be careful, Cobber. I am not a patient man."

Cobber laughed. "Oh, will you look at the big bully spy!"

Barely inclining his head, Knight looked around the crowded lounge. Then, grabbing his partner by the elbow, he steered him out of the room and into the elevator.

"Where're we going, mate?" asked Cobber congenially.

"*You* are going to your room"—the expression on Knight's face would have melted lead—"where

you will stay. I'll order three pots of black coffee. See to it that you drink it all."

"But, Dick—"

Knight glared at him.

"Oh, all right, mate, all right."

* * *

Captain Snider paused uncertainly before his superior's desk. Taking a deep breath, he forced himself to speak. "Sir," he asked, "do you think there could be something wrong with Lieutenant-Colonel Weinberg?"

Cartwright looked up angrily. "There's nothing wrong with Weinberg," he snapped. "How could there be?"

"Well, sir, you know what happened today in your office. And what with the incident at dinner tonight—"

"There's nothing wrong with him," repeated Cartwright firmly. "The only problem is that my staff seems to have turned into a bunch of hero-worshipping teeny-boppers. I'm just as impressed by Wings Weinberg as everyone else, but this is an air base. Where's your perspective? All that happened tonight is that Lieutenant Jones asked him about his cadet days and Wings got a little embarrassed."

"He almost choked to death on his mashed potatoes," amended Snider. "I don't think that's a normal embarrassed reaction. I think something's troubling him."

"Nonsense. Wings Weinberg is the finest young flyer in the service. Just make sure that your men are made aware of my order: he is not to be upset again!"

3

What do *you* think, Mr. Kitzel?

The next morning Sidney ignored the other room-service trays and went straight to Lawrence Waghorn's suite. Waghorn had had an active night—there were three trays outside the door. Sidney looked both ways down the hall. He was alone. Carefully he produced a sheaf of waxed paper and began to wrap the various cups, saucers and bowls and place them in his pockets.

The only other thing on the trays was a crumpled sheet of typewriter paper. In the middle of a large coffee stain, Sidney's highly-trained eyes picked out a word of staggering significance: *espionage*. His heart began to pound with excitement. He had known there was something suspicious about Waghorn. The man was a spy!

Breathlessly Sidney stuffed the paper inside his shirt and began to clank purposefully towards his own room, pockets bulging. As he approached the elevator Tom appeared, wheeling his own cart.

Tom stifled a gasp of horror at the sight of his

brother, who seemed to have an entire service for twelve stashed about his body. "Sidney, what the heck are you doing? Parson's walking around the place!"

Without waiting for a response, Tom hustled his brother over to a nearby linen closet, opened the door and shoved him inside. There was a high-pitched shriek, followed by sounds of a struggle, smashing dishes and falling objects. Horrified, Tom flung the door open. Out flew Sidney. He landed with a resounding crash on the floor and lay there, stunned.

A timid face peered out of the linen closet.

"Oh, dear, it was you." Miss Fuller ventured out. "I do apologize. Are you hurt?"

"Miss Fuller! What on earth were you doing in the linen closet?"

Miss Fuller checked to see that the coast was clear, then motioned the boys closer. "Spying," she whispered. "Every morning Mr. Kitzel disappears before breakfast. I want to know where he goes. You were right, boys. He's a very suspicious character!"

Tom let out a low moan. "I've got to get to the lobby. Sidney, you clean that up and load the rest of the trays." He ran off.

Sidney rose gingerly to his feet, showering fragments of glass and broken crockery from his pockets. "But Mr. Kitzel didn't steal your purse. We found it, remember?"

"That's beside the point," said Edna Fuller firmly. "You boys really opened my eyes. Things

are not always what they seem, as my father used to say."

It was Sidney's turn to check for possible eavesdroppers. "You're right. Things really aren't what they seem," he said earnestly. "I have reason to believe there is some espionage going on at this hotel."

"Espionage!" exclaimed Miss Fuller. "My goodness! But why? What can anybody be after?"

"This is top secret, you understand," whispered Sidney, thrilled to find an understanding confidante. "There's a military air base just north of here. Someone at this hotel isn't here just for a vacation. He's here to spy on that base."

Miss Fuller drew her breath in sharply. "This sounds like the work of Mr. Kitzel!"

"Well, actually—" began Sidney, somewhat startled.

Miss Fuller's face assumed a look of grim determination. "It's my duty as a citizen to find out what he's up to. I'm with you all the way!" She consulted her watch. "He's late this morning— unless he took another route. Oh, we're dealing with a sly one! I'll check in with you later."

Without another word she jogged off in search of the dangerous Mr. Kitzel.

* * *

Sidney took off his red jacket and shook it. Fragments of broken glass and crockery scattered

across the floor of the twins' room. No finger-
prints there, he reflected glumly. He reached into
his shirt to retrieve the piece of paper he had
taken, the one with the word *espionage* in the
coffee stain. Gone. It must have fallen out during
his struggle with Miss Fuller.

He sat down on his bed to think. Waghorn was
definitely a spy. That was obvious. And the air
base was the target. That was obvious too. But
that was all he knew. What he didn't know was
who Waghorn was working with, and that was
vitally important. He would have to intensify his
surveillance. It was time to plant one of his new
electronic listening devices on Waghorn, and
maybe one in his room. In the meantime he'd
write letters to the RCMP and the Department
of National Defence, warning them about Lawrence Waghorn. His face grew thoughtful. Perhaps even a letter to the Prime Minister. . . .

* * *

At Table 19 Mr. Kitzel sat innocently eating his
borscht under the suspicious eye of Miss Fuller.

"Well, Mr. Kitzel," she said conversationally,
"you seem to be very hungry. Had an active
morning?"

"Oh, yes," he replied. "I had a game of shuffleboard and a dip in the pool, and then I played a
little pinochle in the card room."

"You meet a lot of interesting people at a hotel
like this," Miss Fuller went on, her eyes narrow-

ing. "For instance, it's a wonderful place for a spy to hang out."

Bert Cobber began to choke wildly, spraying soup everywhere. Richard Knight reached over and whacked him on the back. Cobber stopped choking, and the purple hue began fading from his complexion. He grabbed his water glass and drank noisily.

"A spy?" said Lawrence Waghorn with keen interest. "What would a spy do here?" He had been grilling himself about that since before his arrival.

"Well," said Miss Fuller, her attention still focused on Mr. Kitzel, who in turn was concerned only with his borscht, "there's an air base right next to the hotel."

Cobber began to choke again.

This time Knight ignored him. "What an interesting idea," he said with cool politeness.

"It sure is!" cried Lawrence Waghorn. His lunch unfinished, he leaped out of his chair and hurried out of the dining room, heading for his typewriter.

"You certainly seem to have quite an imagination, madam," said Knight innocently.

"But, Dick!" blurted Cobber. He was kicked sharply under the table.

"Oh, I don't know," said Miss Fuller sweetly. "It's just a logical assumption to make. This is a perfect place for anyone who might want to spy on the base to make his headquarters. What do you think, Mr. Kitzel?"

Mr. Kitzel looked up, spoon poised, and licked his lips. "I think this is the best borscht I've ever tasted!"

* * *

"Mate," said Bert Cobber urgently as he and Knight teed off at the first hole, "that old girl's onto us! Do you think she's a cop?"

Characteristically, Knight barely moved as he did a thorough scan of the surrounding area. No one was within earshot.

"Cobber, do learn to lower your voice. If I wanted to alert everyone to our intentions, I would take out an ad in the Sunday paper."

Knight executed a lithe swing. His ball soared down the fairway and landed in perfect position for his second shot.

"You're not listening, Dick! If the old lady's a cop and she's sniffed out our game we could go to jail, you know!"

"I have no intention of going to jail."

"But aren't we going to rub her out?"

Knight laughed shortly. "Cobber, I do not make a practice of 'rubbing out' old ladies simply because they have overactive imaginations. Just leave Miss Fuller to me and concern yourself with keeping a low profile until such time as I require your services as a pilot."

Cobber's attention immediately shifted. "What plane am I going to be flying, eh, Dick? Can I know now?" He swung mightily, sending tee and

ball bouncing down the fairway. He and Knight began to walk.

"All right, Cobber, but this is absolutely secret. The plane is called the Osiris HE2. It is the most advanced aircraft to date, and is presently being readied for testing at Trillium Base."

"But, Dick," Cobber protested, "I couldn't fly a thing like that without the manual. Even Wings Weinberg would need a manual, and he's the greatest pilot ever."

"You'll have your flight manual in time," replied Knight. "Strange you should mention Weinberg. He's the pilot who was chosen to test the Osiris. He's at Trillium right now."

"You're kidding! Wings? At Trillium? Wow! We used to be great friends when we were cadets together. Will he ever be glad to see me!"

Knight smiled thinly. "Cobber, need I remind you that Lieutenant-Colonel Weinberg is on the other side?"

Cobber looked taken aback. "Yeah. What a shame. Imagine—me and Wings on different sides. Who would have thought it? Man, we were good buddies!"

* * *

"So how are you doing on the Osiris flight manual?" Captain Snider asked Colonel Weinberg. The two were seated at a table in the Officers' Club.

Wings smiled, showing a perfect set of white

34

teeth, and his blue eyes brightened. "Fine," he said. "It's a fascinating plane. The details are a little sketchy, of course. It's my job to fill them in after the test flight. I'm really looking forward to that."

"So is Colonel Cartwright," said Snider, grinning. "As a matter of fact, he's looking forward to it so much that he's scared to death. This has to be the world's greatest test flight because it's at Trillium. He won't hear of it any other way. He's acting just like a ca— I mean—uh—like someone who hasn't been in the service for very long."

"Uh—yeah," Weinberg said nervously. His calm returned immediately. "Yes. Well, I'll do my best."

"I'm sure your best will be incredible, Colonel Weinberg," said Snider.

"Oh, call me Wings," said The Legend.

"My name's Jack." Snider was pink with pleasure. "Oh, wow, I can't believe it! This is exactly how I'm not supposed to react, but you're really my hero. I feel like a cadet again and—oops—"

Once again Weinberg had turned pale. "Why is it that all anybody ever wants to talk about around here is being a cadet? I hated being a cadet! I never talk about my cadet days! I never even *think* about my cadet days! Never! *Never!*"

As Snider led The Legend out of the Officers' Club, he was still repeating the word "never."

*   *   *

35

Lawrence Waghorn leaned against a post on the hotel's front porch, staring off into space and praying vaguely for inspiration. He was depressed. How was he supposed to meet such a short deadline? So there was a spy, a hotel and an air base. So what? What came next?

At the other end of the porch hovered Sidney Weston, inconspicuously watching and waiting. In his right hand he clutched a small electronic listening device.

From behind a large juniper bush at the side of the porch Tom Weston cautiously raised his head, scouting out the scene. Sidney had been acting peculiar and, his drive for self-preservation activated, Tom had followed him here. Sidney was definitely up to no good. And just what did he have in his right hand?

Tom watched in horror as Sidney approached Waghorn and passed him closely, dropping a small black object into the pocket of his safari jacket. Waghorn still glared straight ahead, apparently unaware that anything had happened. He seemed abstracted. Tom moved out from behind the bush, walked purposefully across the porch and brushed past him, removing the contents of his jacket pocket. Sidney wasn't the only one with spy skills, he thought in triumph.

He ran around the corner of the building, stopped and opened his hand. There was Sidney's electronic listening device—and a large wad of twenty-dollar bills. Breathless with the horror of what he had done, Tom threw Sidney's bug into

the bushes and raced around to the front porch. Waghorn was gone.

*   *   *

Sidney stood by the letter box in the hotel lobby, feeding his outgoing mail into the slot. It was a good night's work, he thought with satisfaction. He had alerted six agencies to the dangers of Lawrence Waghorn. As he dropped his letters one by one into the slot, he ticked them off mentally: the Ontario Provincial Police, the RCMP, the office of the Prime Minister, the Department of National Defence, NATO and Norad.

"You seem to have a passion for writing letters, Tom," came Mr. Parson's voice from behind him.

Sidney wheeled. "Uh—I'm Sidney, sir. I was just writing to some of my—uh—relatives."

"You must spend a lot of time on such a mammoth project. Do we not provide you with enough work to do here at Pine Grove?"

"I write the letters in my spare time, sir."

"See that you do," said Mr. Parson. "I've got my eye on you two Weston boys and—are you listening to me?"

Sidney was watching Lawrence Waghorn as he walked up to them.

"Mr. Parson, I appear to have lost some money. What should I do?"

Parson beamed. "I may already have the answer to your problem, Mr. Waghorn. Just a while

ago Tom here turned in some money at the desk."

"It must have been my brother, sir."

"Pardon me?"

"I'm Sidney, remember? It must have been my brother Tom who handed in the money."

"Quiet, Weston," hissed the manager. "Come this way, Mr. Waghorn. We'll see if this money is yours."

* * *

Richard Knight, clad entirely in black, his face darkened, slipped like a shadow across the Pine Grove golf course towards the fence surrounding Trillium Air Base.

The guard would be increased because of the presence of the Osiris, he thought to himself, but not conspicuously so. Too much obvious security would arouse curiosity. So it shouldn't be hard to get in. Still, one could not be too careful.

Suddenly he stopped, sniffing the air like a bloodhound. Melting into the shadows, he crouched by a bush for a few seconds, then emerged and said in a soft voice, "Cobber, go back to bed."

Cobber stepped out from behind a tree. "Boy, mate, you are amazing! How'd you know it was me?"

"Anybody else following me would not have been quite so obvious about it," said Knight coldly. "Be grateful that I recognized your

38

clumsy footsteps. The last person who followed me never reported back to his superiors."

"Sorry, mate, I didn't mean to scare you. I just wanted to see where you were going. I want to be in on this."

"Cobber, this is not amateur night. Go back to bed. And *never* attempt to interfere with my activities again."

"Yeah, yeah, mate, I'm going. Don't get excited."

4

A one-man doomsday machine

While his brother was still on morning duty, Sidney worked furiously at his desk. Beneath a high-intensity lamp and a magnifying glass lay a much-used sheet of carbon paper. It had been removed from Waghorn's wastebasket that morning and spirited into Sidney's pocket during his service rounds.

Sidney stared intently through the glass. The carbon had been typed over many times and was nearly impossible to read. His heart began to pound as he came to a clear portion in the jumble and read: *Espionage activity based at resort hotel.* The jumble resumed. Below that he could make out *Object: spying on military secrets at adjacent air base.* Then the jumble got even worse. The next legible thing was the last line, located about halfway down the page. It read, *Plan Stage One: observation by night. Agent:,* and then nothing.

Sidney's mind began to race. This was proof

positive—Waghorn *was* a spy! Quivering with excitement, he affixed a date sticker to the sheet of carbon paper, rolled his bed away from the wall, removed a section of panelling and swung open a piece of wallboard. He filed away the incriminating carbon, satisfied that it was perfectly safe there along with the rest of his files, notes and photographs. Tom would never find it.

Setting everything back to normal, he walked over to his bed lamp and removed the shade. It was time to check on Waghorn via the listening device he had planted yesterday. He flicked a hidden switch and placed a small jack in his ear. There were two voices, both male, and loud unidentifiable noises punctuating the background. Neither voice belonged to Waghorn. Sidney listened intently.

*　　*　　*

Two members of the Pine Grove gardening staff were working in the flower bed by the front porch.

"Seems to me these beds need work every day," complained one man.

"It's that dog, Blackie," said the other. "He digs them up all the time."

"You mean the retriever?"

"Yeah, the retriever. He's a killer when it comes to flowers."

"Right. Hey—look at that." He pointed to a black object in the earth. "Is that a bug?"

"Biggest darn bug I've ever seen!" said the other man. "Probably feeding on my tulip bulbs." He raised his shovel and smashed it down on the object.

* * *

"Ow!" A shocked Sidney Weston wrenched the jack from his ear and held the side of his head gingerly. As the ringing began to fade, his keen mind started processing the information he had just taken in. The signal had been very faint at first. He thought he'd heard the word "dog," but dismissed that. Then the sound had improved and the two voices had spoken about someone called "Retriever." They'd even referred to him as a killer! Then they'd located the listening device and destroyed it.

Sidney frowned. They had obviously recognized the device—they'd called it a bug. That meant that Waghorn's people, whoever they were, knew now that someone was watching them. They couldn't possibly know it was Sidney, but still they would probably be much more careful after this incident. He would have to watch himself too, he reflected with a slight quiver. They had said this Retriever was a killer!

A key in the lock signified that Tom had returned. Quickly Sidney put the lamp back to normal and was lounging casually on his bed when his brother entered the room.

"Hi, Tom," he said nonchalantly.

"Hi. Here's your pay cheque. Do you know what this means?"

"What?"

"It means that you're going into town to buy some clothes. Get moving. You have to be back by dinner."

"Gee," said Sidney reluctantly, "I hate to spend it. I'm saving up for some things."

"What is it this time? A home autopsy kit? A ballistics lab? An atomic bomb? Forget it, Sidney. It's to everyone's advantage that you don't get any more of that junk. And you *need* clothes, because after today you're not borrowing any more of mine!"

"Oh, all right," sighed Sidney.

* * *

Mr. Kitzel, resplendent in his blue Olympic jogging suit, loped along the golf course, keeping close to the fence to stay out of the golfers' way. He glanced nervously over his shoulder. Yes, she was still there, that Fuller woman. What did she want from him? Oh, no! Not that! Could she be in love with him? She'd been following him around lately—not too close, but still following. That could be it. And this vacation could have been so wonderful for him—fine weather, good food, excellent recreation, comfortable accommodation, superb entertainment. Why her?

I've got to give her the slip, he decided. Glancing over his shoulder again, he noticed that she

was momentarily distracted by an enraged golfer whose ball she had accidentally kicked. Quickly he dashed behind a clump of bushes and crouched there, breathing hard.

"Yoo-hoo, Mr. Kitzel!" With a sinking heart, Mr. Kitzel looked up. Miss Fuller was standing over him. "There you are! What are you doing out here so close to the air base?"

Mr. Kitzel stood up, trying to assume an air of nonchalance. "I was—uh—resting. Yes, resting from my jogging."

"Tired already? You haven't jogged very far."

"Well, I was going to quit anyway," said Mr. Kitzel, his morning spoiled. "It's almost lunch time."

"Lunch isn't for another two hours," Miss Fuller pressed him. "Why, you have time to do almost anything. Even break into the air base," she added suggestively.

Mr. Kitzel looked blank. "Why would I want to do that?"

"Oh, no reason." Miss Fuller inhaled deeply. He was a sly one, this Mr. Kitzel.

*   *   *

Captain Snider sat with Wings Weinberg in the test pilot's room in the Officers' Quarters. Wings' veneer of unflappable calm was blown to pieces. His eyes were glazed, and his pallor was startling. The Legend was pouring himself a triple scotch with shaking hand.

"I guess you wouldn't know it to look at me, but I've got problems."

"Really?" asked Snider tactfully.

Wings nodded fervently. "I've been dreading this day for years, hoping it would never come, hoping the past would be buried forever. But now all anybody cares about is my cadet days—I don't understand it! Is everybody around here nuts? They wouldn't talk about cadet days if they'd been through what I've been through!"

Snider nodded sympathetically. "I suppose you crashed a few times."

Wings looked surprised. "Me? Never. But they gave me this flying partner named Bert Cobber!" He shuddered. "I'll never forget that name! Bert Cobber was the craziest pilot I've ever seen in my life! The guy cost us more planes than the Second World War! And he was *my* partner! *My* life depended on him! Every night I'd have nightmares about Bert Cobber getting me killed, and the next day they'd all come true! I swear to you that I'm alive today *in spite of* Bert Cobber!"

Snider laughed out loud, mostly in nervous relief. "Is that all?"

"What do you mean *'Is that all?'*" shouted Wings. "You never knew him! He was a one-man doomsday machine, a flying Krakatoa! He was death from above! And he haunts me!"

"Don't worry, Wings," soothed Snider, holding back his laughter in an attempt to look serious. "This guy Cobber must be dead by now if he was such a lousy pilot."

"Lousy? He was a great pilot. That's how he got to be my partner—we were the top two in the class. But nuts! He had some weird kind of faith that somehow he'd get through anything. And *I* had to fly with him! And *I* haven't got that kind of faith!"

"Where is he now?"

Wings shrugged. "Who knows? He could be anywhere." He looked nervously at the ceiling. "Do you realize he could be up there somewhere right now? No one is safe!"

"Come on, Wings," chided Snider. "Isn't that a little paranoid? Your cadet days are a long way off, and so is this guy Cobber."

*   *   *

Richard Knight sat in quiet reflection as Bert Cobber marched around the room, bubbling with conversation.

"Oh, boy, Dick, you should have seen us, me and Wings. We were a great team. Of course, he wasn't 'Wings' back then. We called him Whiny—not only because of his name, but because he was always whining and complaining before every flight. You'd have thought he hated flying. But, boy, he was a great pilot."

"I am not interested, Cobber."

"We did everything together," Cobber went on. "Why, did I ever tell you about the time I saved his life?"

"Many times," said Knight absently.

"We were on a drill up in the Northwest Territories and Wings was lying on the ice with two broken ribs, freezing to death. There were wolves all around. I can still hear them howling."

"Last time it was a family of polar bears," said Knight, not looking up.

"Let me tell you, mate, it was pretty rough. But I got Wings back into the plane and halfway home before we ran out of gas."

Knight cocked an eyebrow. "Oh, a new ending. How does this one turn out?"

"We crash-landed outside of Thunder Bay and hitched a ride the rest of the way with a travelling circus troupe. Man, was Wings ever grateful to me! He owed me so much he was embarrassed about it. He didn't even want to see me or talk to me."

"I know the feeling."

Cobber sighed. "I'll bet Wings tells that story often."

* * *

"You know, Wings," said Snider, "you're the greatest test pilot in the world. You can't just spend all your life worrying about some guy who's probably dead by now anyway."

Wings finished off his second triple scotch and went to pour himself another. "You're just lucky it wasn't you. Why, once we were flying a drill mission to the Northwest Territories, and Cobber was still hung over from his weekend pass. The

guy couldn't keep a straight line or follow a map, and we were running low on fuel. Then he dipped too low over a peak and ripped my door off. I fell out! Ten metres! I dropped into a snowbank or I'd have been killed! As it was, I broke two ribs. I crawled out of the snowbank half dead, and the idiot almost landed on me! He grabbed me and threw me into the plane, screaming something about bears and wolves!"

"At least he got you home."

"Then we ran out of gas," Wings went on bitterly. "Cobber called it crash-landing. I call it crashing! We finally hitchhiked home with a circus. They let us ride in the elephant wagon." He shuddered. "And you want to know why I can't bear to think about my cadet days!"

"Did Cobber ever graduate?" asked Snider.

"Of course. He was second in the class. After that I never saw him again. I guess I've been lucky so far."

"And that's all?"

"All? *All?* I could go on forever! But what would you expect from a guy whose good-luck piece was a feather? Some people have coins, rabbits' feet—Cobber had a metre-and-a-half-long peacock feather! He used to take it on training flights and stick it in my face to make me sneeze!"

"Well, anyway," said Snider, standing up, "you've finally told your story. You got it off your chest and now you can forget it and go on ɔm here. Don't you feel better already?"

Sidney's face brightened. "It was a real bargain —only eighty dollars."

"Eighty dollars? But Sidney, you only *had* eighty dollars! What are you going to do for clothes?"

"Oh. Sorry, but I couldn't pass this up."

Tom sat down wearily at the desk and prepared pen and paper. "I'll write Mom and ask her to mail you some of your clothes. I should have known better than to assume you'd actually buy what you were sent for."

Sidney's sharp eyes glanced under the bureau. "Hey, what's all that stuff doing there?"

"Hiding," said Tom bitterly. "From you."

*   *   *

Walter Parson came strolling into the pool area, a large black dog at his heels.

"Ah, good afternoon, Mr. Waghorn. Are you enjoying your stay?"

"Yes, very much so," said Waghorn. It was a lie. He had just come from a telephone conversation with his producer. The chief was impatient. Waghorn had barely started the outline for his story and was bogged down and depressed. The only idea he did have he had stolen from that Fuller woman.

Parson looked up at the sky and breathed deeply. "The weather is wonderful." He glanced down at his dog, who was sniffing around a lady sunbathing near the pool. "Heel, Blackie." The

dog responded immediately. "You know you're not allowed to go around bothering the guests."

"A beautiful dog," commented Waghorn.

"Oh, thank you," said Parson proudly. "He's a purebred Labrador retriever."

The P.A. system crackled. "Mr. Parson, please come to the lobby. Mr. Parson, to the lobby."

The hotel manager slipped the handle of the dog's leash around a small tree. "You just wait here, Blackie. I'll be right back." And he hurried off towards the lobby.

Lawrence Waghorn stroked Blackie's long, streamlined back. "What a lovely dog."

*   *   *

Carrying a load of towels for the use of the pool guests, Sidney strode down the path from the laundry. He stopped short behind the lifeguard tower, his jaw dropping. There under a tree stood Lawrence Waghorn, patting a large black dog.

"A Labrador *retriever!*" gasped Sidney, jamming his fist into his mouth to stifle his words. The gears in his trained mind began to turn furiously. Instantly he recalled the conversation between Waghorn's two associates before they had destroyed the listening device. They had been talking about the "retriever," the "killer." He'd thought he heard the word "dog"—and here was Waghorn with a Labrador retriever!

Was it feasible? Could a crafty agent and a specially trained dog head an entire espionage or-

ganization intent on the air base? It seemed likely—almost positive. An athletic dog like that could easily jump the high fence and steal undetected practically anywhere on the base. Waghorn would seldom need to risk his own neck in spying activities. He could simply send the dog out to do the work. It was fiendishly brilliant!

But— Sidney's mind sliced at the problem. Without the dog Waghorn would be crippled, the plot would bog down and the organization would be hurt. The dog must be stopped.

Waghorn walked away, leaving Blackie alone. Sidney looked about. Everyone was facing the pool—he would never get a better opportunity. Could he control a trained animal that size? He took a deep breath. He had to try.

Sidney ran up to the tree, grabbed the leash, looked around quickly and dashed off, the dog loping along beside him. He entered the hotel through one of the staff entrances, went up via the freight elevator, dashed down the corridor to his room and hustled the dog inside. Blackie wagged his tail and whined. Suddenly he lunged for Sidney, placing a great paw on each shoulder and licking the boy's face. Then he jumped down and began inspecting the room.

Slowly Sidney's face lost the deathly white shade it had taken on, and his heart started beating again. For some reason this dangerous creature seemed to like him.

He checked his watch. He was on duty for another hour. He had to get back to work before

he was missed. Letting himself out, he carefully locked the dog in the room and went down to check the duty roster to see what he was to do next.

"*Pssst!*"

Sidney looked around.

"*Pssst!*" A hand reached out and pulled him into a telephone alcove. "There you are, dear," Miss Fuller whispered. "I have to talk to you about"—she looked around furtively—"Mr. Kitzel."

"Well—uh—" Sidney stammered.

"This morning I caught him skulking in the bushes around the air base fence. He said he was resting!"

"Actually, Mr. Kitzel hasn't really ever—"

"I'm *sure* he's guilty," Miss Fuller overrode him with firm conviction. "Although I have no idea how that fat old fool will ever get over the fence."

"Well, I've figured out the part about the fence," whispered Sidney. "I believe a trained dog is being used—a Labrador retriever. But don't worry. I've got him on ice for a while."

"That sneaky old man!" Miss Fuller exploded.

"Ma'am, I don't think Mr. Kitzel has anything to do with—"

"A dog!" she repeated. "How terribly clever of him! I'll have to double my surveillance. We can't rest until Mr. Kitzel is safely behind bars."

"Uh—yes, Ma'am."

* * *

"Sidney," called Tom, letting himself into their room after work that afternoon, "did you hear the news? Mr. Parson's dog has been stolen. It's a black Labrador—"

From behind the bathroom door Blackie erupted like a bomb, pinning Tom against the wall.

"—retriever," he finished in a terrified whisper.

The dog sniffed at Tom and growled menacingly. Panic-stricken, Tom scrambled up the bookshelves as though they were stairs. The dog snapped after him, removing a large piece of fabric from the seat of his trousers. Tom sat gasping on the top shelf, his eyes fixed on the menacing creature below.

"Help!"

Sidney looked in the door. "Tom? Is something wrong?"

"Sidney, *run!*"

Tail wagging, the creature trotted over to Sidney, whining happily and licking the boy's hand.

"Come on down, Tom. Don't tell me you're afraid of him. He's as gentle as a lamb."

"He doesn't like me! He almost bit me in half! Sidney, *what* are you doing with Mr. Parson's dog?"

Sidney goggled. "This is Parson's dog?"

"Yes. His name is Blackie and he was stolen from the pool area today. Why would you steal a dog?"

"I can't tell you."

"What do you mean you can't tell me? If we

get caught with him we're both fired! Mr. Parson is freaking out over this dog!"

"Did you see anyone with Parson?" Sidney asked suspiciously.

Tom's heart sank. "Mr. Waghorn," he admitted. "He was the last one to see Blackie before he disappeared."

Sidney smiled inwardly. Just as he'd suspected —Mr. Parson was in on this too. Parson was pretending to own Waghorn's dog to keep people from associating the dog and Waghorn.

"Sidney, you've got to give it back! Tell Parson you found it somewhere! Our jobs are on the line!"

"I can't do that," said Sidney solemnly.

"Well then, I'll do it!" Tom reached for the leash. Blackie snapped at his hand and Tom withdrew swiftly. "Why does he hate me and love you? We're exactly alike. And *you* stole him!"

Sidney shrugged. "When you're in the room I'll tie him to my bed or something so he can't get at you."

"Sidney, if you had to kidnap a dog, why Parson's? Why not someone else's dog? The hotel kennel is full of dogs owned by nice people who aren't our boss and who don't hate us already!"

"It had to be this way," said Sidney cryptically. "I can't say any more."

Tom sighed. If he tried to return the dog by himself it would tear him apart. "How long do we have to keep him?" he demanded sourly. Why was life so complicated?

"Until it's safe," replied Sidney, "I'll tell you."

Resignedly Tom sat down on his bed. What was Sidney up to? What could he possibly suspect this dog of doing? The more he thought about it, the more bewildered he became. He had been hoping to keep tabs on his brother, but things were getting out of hand. Between this dog and that enormous contraption Sidney had bought— oh, no! Where was it? He looked around the room. How could Sidney have hidden a thing of that size in their little room, especially when everything else he owned was hidden somewhere too?

Tom frowned at his brother, who was sitting on the floor absently stroking Blackie's fur. Well, he decided, if he was going to keep up with Sidney he'd just have to work a little harder. He had obviously gotten a little behind.

At the same time, the evidence he had collected was floating around in Sidney's head. There was still a long way to go in this investigation. As soon as possible he would put his new equipment into use. And as soon as he had time he would write more letters to keep the government agencies up to date. This time he'd notify the President of the United States as well. He might be concerned with this too.

* * *

At Table 19 Mr. Kitzel was attacking a second huge bowl of matzo-ball soup, smacking his lips appreciatively.

"Say, I wonder who stole the manager's dog," said Bert Cobber sociably.

"I hope they find him," put in Lawrence Waghorn. "He's a beautiful animal."

"Yes, and dogs can be very *useful* creatures too," added Edna Fuller, staring at Mr. Kitzel. "For example, a dog could be a tremendous boon to a spy."

Casually, Knight handed Cobber a napkin to choke into.

"How so?" asked Waghorn, interested. This woman had started his script; maybe she could add something to it.

"Well," she said, not taking her eyes for a second from the oblivious Mr. Kitzel, "just pretend you have a spy after something on the air base."

Knight handed Cobber another napkin.

"And," Miss Fuller went on, "rather than constantly risking his own neck, he trains a dog to"—she paused—"*retrieve* whatever he's after. A dog is more athletic than a man and would have no trouble at all getting over the fence. It just seems logical."

"Dick, can I talk to you—" began Cobber.

"That's a great idea!" cried Waghorn, jumping out of his chair. On the dead run, he tore out of the dining room and upstairs towards his typewriter.

Knight displayed a thin smile. "It does seem extremely logical, madam."

"Dick—" began Cobber warningly.

"It certainly seems obvious to me," Miss Fuller agreed. "What do you think, Mr. Kitzel?"

58

"In all my life," mumbled Mr. Kitzel, mouth full, "I have never tasted better matzo-ball soup!"

* * *

As a drifting cloud obscured the light of the moon, Richard Knight silently slipped out of the sleeping hotel and melted into the shadows of the grounds. He would not be followed this time, he remarked inwardly. Not an hour ago he had slipped some knockout drops into Cobber's drink. The pilot would be dead to the world until morning.

As for Miss Fuller, Knight could not quite understand her obsession with spies. But one thing seemed obvious. He and Cobber were in no danger from her. She seemed intent only on that poor Mr. Kitzel. Knight smiled to himself. Mr. Kitzel's only dangerous activity appeared to be a gross tendency to overeat.

The mission must be taken seriously, of course, but it certainly seemed to have its amusing aspects.

He turned his eyes ahead towards the air base.

5

Dear Mr. Weston

Blackie peered with mild interest over Sidney's shoulder as the boy stared intently through his magnifying glass. He was examining the latest piece of carbon paper from Waghorn's room-service tray, picked up just a few minutes before.

"I was right!" he exclaimed triumphantly to the dog. What he could make of the carbon read: *Agent Retriever is a dog being used by the head of the organization. The organization has a number of dogs (known as the Z-series) specially trained in espionage. The one called Retriever is Z-2. Z-4 and Z-5 are standing by.* He turned to Blackie. "So that's who you are, Z-2!" Blackie wagged his tail benignly.

He must be very well trained, thought Sidney. He doesn't even budge when his code name is called. Gee, he seemed so harmless—it was hard to think of this dog as a killer.

Suddenly Blackie growled and bared his teeth. Sidney wheeled to find that Tom had quietly let

himself into the room. Quickly Sidney whipped the sheet of carbon paper under his pillow.

"Hold back that monster," said Tom, reaching for his fresh uniform. "We've got to get to work."

"You go first," said Sidney nonchalantly. "I'll be down in a few seconds."

"No," said Tom stubbornly. "You go first. You're the one who's ready. I'm not dressed yet."

"I'll wait for you."

"Is there any reason why you don't want to leave this room?" Tom demanded.

"Well—no."

"Then go."

Very reluctantly, moving as slowly as he could, Sidney closed the dog in the washroom and headed for the door. "Aren't you coming?"

"I'm not ready yet," said Tom, who had been putting on the same sock for the past five minutes.

Finally Sidney left the room, deploring the fact that he had not had time to file away the piece of carbon paper or hide his magnifying glass.

Inside, Tom pounced on Sidney's pillow and grabbed the carbon. What was this and where had Sidney acquired it? He squinted through the magnifying glass. Who could possibly read this? It had been typed to shreds. He stared at it from various angles. Wait a minute—he could make out *dog* and *Z-2*. Suddenly the words sprang off the page at him: *specially trained in espionage*.

Tom began to feel sick. Surely whoever had written this couldn't mean that Blackie was Z-2,

a spy dog! Could he? The dog was mean enough, but all kidding aside...

"Hey, you," he called into the washroom, "are you Z-2?"

Angry snarling came in response.

Tom evaluated the situation. Sidney had kidnapped a dog named Z-2. Someone had typed something saying Z-2 was a spy dog, and Sidney obviously believed it. The thing was, how could this be a spy dog when everybody knew full well that it belonged to Mr. Parson? And who had typed that carbon? Just what was going on here?

Tom's bewildered eyes fell upon the clock. He was five minutes late for work already. Hurriedly he stuffed the carbon paper back under Sidney's pillow, finished dressing and rushed from the room.

* * *

"Wow, mate, I sure had a great sleep last night. Slept like a baby. That drink you bought me sure had a lot of kick."

Knight produced a large manila envelope. "Here you are, Cobber. The flight manual for the Osiris HE2."

Cobber's eyes opened wide. "Where'd you get it?"

Knight smiled thinly. "I paid your friend Weinberg a visit last night and photographed his."

"How is Wings?" asked Cobber cautiously.

"I broke into his room," Knight explained patiently. "It was not a social call. I did not enquire about his health."

"You didn't hurt him, did you?"

"It was not necessary. Your friend Weinberg is a very heavy sleeper."

"Funny. He had terrible insomnia when we were together."

"I'm not surprised," said Knight. "It was probably the ringing in his ears."

"What was that? What did you say, eh, Dick?"

"Never mind, Cobber. Now, pay attention. These photographs comprise the pages of the flight manual. Commit every line, figure and legend to memory. And don't let them out of your sight. Possession of this information is unbelievably incriminating."

"Yeah, yeah, mate, I'll be careful."

* * *

"Sidney Weston."

Tom wheeled to face Mr. Parson. Wrong again, he thought, but who am I to argue? "Yes, sir?"

"Some mail arrived for you today," said the manager coldly. "Normally it would have been deposited in your mail slot, but in this case I thought I'd better hand it over personally. Why is it that the Royal Canadian Mounted Police, the Ontario Provincial Police and the Ministry of Transportation have all seen fit to write to you at this hotel?"

Tom was stunned, unable to reply. Sidney had been writing letters again! Tom could not even confess at this point that he was not Sidney.

"Well," said Mr. Parson, his tone menacing, "I await your explanation."

Miss Fuller popped out from behind the potted palm where she had been lurking, watching Mr. Kitzel read his afternoon paper. "Mr. Parson, I think that's totally uncalled-for!"

"Pardon me, madam?"

"Just because the boy works for you doesn't give you the right to bully him—*or* to censor his mail."

Parson was flustered. "My dear madam, noth ing was further from my mind. I was merely concerned that Sidney might be in trouble."

"If he's in trouble and he doesn't want to tell you, then it's none of your business. I take a dim view of hotel managers who abuse the hired help. Besides, any fool can see that that's not Sidney. It's Tom."

Mr. Parson muttered his apologies and retreated hastily to the desk.

Miss Fuller dragged Tom into a telephone alcove. She glanced at Mr. Kitzel to assure herself that he was out of earshot.

"You *are* Tom, aren't you?"

"Yes, Ma'am."

She breathed a sigh of relief. "I wasn't sure. Has Sidney been keeping you up to date on my Kitzel investigation?"

Tom looked sick. "Well—"

"I want you to get those letters to Sidney right away. I must know what's in them about Mr. Kitzel."

"Uh—ma'am—actually—"

"I have to go," said Miss Fuller suddenly. She strolled off nonchalantly, following Mr. Kitzel out into the sunshine.

* * *

"So I said to the general, 'Your new Rigel X-22 rides like a Checker Cab on a dirt road—sir.'"

There was laughter and applause all round the table.

"Wings, that's priceless," said Colonel Cartwright. "I always wondered why they never developed the Rigel."

Wings grinned. "I'd hate to be the pilot who had to get it started on a cold morning. What a bucket!"

There was more laughter. Some of the younger pilots were positively glowing with admiration.

"Was that the worst plane you ever tested?" asked a young lieutenant.

"By no means," said Weinberg. "That was one of the better ones. The worst was the Carroll-RIC. It bounced like a beach ball and never got off the ground."

"What was the best?" asked Captain Snider.

"The Water Moc was a sweet one," replied Wings, "but the Osiris is going to be beautiful."

"Right!" Colonel Cartwright was pink with pleasure.

"That reminds me of another incident," Wings went on. "When I was testing the Vector-ML..."

As Wings related the story to an enraptured audience, Cartwright nudged his security chief. "You see, Snider? When you stop embarrassing the guy, he's incredible! What a personality!"

Snider grinned knowingly. "You were right, sir."

* * *

Warily Tom let himself into the room. "Blackie," he called softly.

The answer was a malicious growl. The dog was lying on Sidney's bed with his head turned towards Tom, an unkind expression in his large, dark eyes.

With a watchful eye on the animal, Tom tossed Sidney's letters onto the desk. I've got to get rid of this dog, he thought. He'll get us both fired—if he doesn't kill me first. He swung the door wide, peered out into the deserted hall and motioned with his arm.

"Come on, Blackie. Out you go."

Still growling, Blackie jumped off the bed and stood on the floor, eying Tom with suspicion.

"Come on. You're free. Get out of here." He clapped his hands twice.

Casually, tossing a nasty glance at Tom, Blackie trotted out the door and down the hall.

Tom slammed the door and leaned against it, weak with relief. Sidney could complain all he wanted to. Blackie was gone.

That taken care of, he turned to Sidney's mail. Here was a moral dilemma. Should he open Sidney's letters in the interest of saving their jobs? If he read them, he would have a better idea of what his brother was up to. But then Sidney would be angry, and rightly so. Not only that, but he would become even more secretive. Perhaps Tom should destroy the letters before Sidney got a chance to read them. That would save a great deal of grief for everyone involved. But it wasn't right to interfere with the mail, was it? It wasn't even legal. Yet if Sidney got those letters, who could say what the outcome might be?

The sound of a key in the lock solved the problem. Sidney came into the room, tossed his uniform jacket onto his bed and opened the bathroom door.

"Where's the dog?"

"I let him go," said Tom evenly. "He isn't yours."

"You what?" Sidney was distraught. "You have to understand that when I do something I have a good reason for doing it, even though security sometimes forces me into secrecy! Tom, how could you? This is terrible!"

"It's not terrible," corrected Tom. "It's very good. Service boys aren't supposed to have stolen dogs roaming around their rooms."

"But, Tom—"

He was interrupted by an odd scratching sound.

Tom opened the door. In bounded Blackie,

hurling himself joyously at Sidney, pinning him to the desk with his large paws and licking his face wildly. Then he jumped down, tossed a contemptuous bark at Tom and went to sleep on the floor by Sidney's bed.

"Oh, no!" moaned Tom. "Z-2 is back!"

Sidney was instantly alert. "Where did you hear that name?"

Tom wished he hadn't said anything. "What name?"

"Z-2. You called the dog Z-2. Where did you hear that?"

Tom thought hard. "Uh—you called him that."

"No, I didn't. I would never make a slip like that."

"You were talking in your sleep," said Tom, pleased at having come up with a plausible lie.

That could be true, thought Sidney. He made a mental note to do something about talking in his sleep. Perhaps staying awake . . .

"Anyway," he said, "you shouldn't say Z-2 outside this room. If you do, you could be in very grave danger."

"What kind of danger?"

"That's all I can say." Sidney reached into the inside pocket of his jacket and produced two large sirloin steaks wrapped in foil. "Here you go, Z-2. Here's your dinner."

"You stole those!" accused Tom as Blackie shook himself awake and wolfed down the steaks. "That's twenty bucks worth of meat! Couldn't you get him anything cheaper—like dog food?"

"Well, no. I had to run because Parson saw me."

"Parson saw you? What did he say?"

Sidney thought back. "He said, 'Tom, get out of the meat locker.'"

Tom shook his head to clear it. "Sidney, you're impossible!" He lay back on his bed. "There's some mail for you on the desk."

"Mail?" Sidney pounced on the letters. He opened the one from the Ministry of Transportation first. It read:

Dear Mr. Weston,

Welcome back! All the guys at the office have been making bets about when we'd hear from you again. It's been two months since you inquired about the Sunday School bus you decided was smuggling cocaine, and we've missed you. The poor innocent fellow you're out to get this time, licence number LKW 551, is a Mr. Lawrence K. Waghorn of 17 Baldwin Crescent, Toronto, Ontario. We sincerely pity him.
Yours truly,
Dave

"What does it say?" asked Tom, curious in spite of himself. "Miss Fuller wants to know what's in there about Mr. Kitzel."

"Nothing," said Sidney. "Mr. Kitzel isn't involved in this."

"Tell *her* that."

Sidney opened the letter from the RCMP.

Dear Mr. Weston,

Hello again. We were beginning to wonder what had happened to you. I guess things have been pretty quiet since the Salvation Army tried to take over the world.

We are sorry, but after much deliberation we have elected not to assign any men to protect Trillium Air Base. We feel that the Forces can protect themselves, and if they can't, who is going to protect the country?

Also, thank you for sending us that shard of broken glass with the fingerprint on it. It was yours. Our mail clerk required four stitches and a tetanus shot.

Relay our condolences to your Mr. Waghorn. We have no idea what unfortunate circumstance (for him) drew him to your ever-watchful attention, but he has no criminal record and his face is not known to us.

Yours sincerely,

Bruce

Hmmm, thought Sidney, Waghorn has no criminal record.

"Let me see one of those," said Tom.

"I'm sorry, Tom, but I can't show you the letters."

Tom muttered something about a lack of trust. He was extremely alarmed at the intensity of Sidney's expression. As Sidney himself would have put it, the investigation was progressing. That meant trouble. There was always trouble

when his brother got to the letter-writing stage. Tom would have to stay on his toes.

Sidney opened the last letter.

> *Dear Mr. Weston,*
>   *Please stop bothering us.*
> *Cordially yours,*
> *The Ontario Provincial Police*

Sidney looked up and scratched his head. It was time for him to warn the air base.

* * *

"Sir," said Corporal Hayes timidly, "I just received the strangest phone call."

"Well, Hayes, speak up. Who was it?"

"Well, it was some strange man—I guess it was a man. He was whispering. Everything happened so fast—I didn't get it all. He—he said there's a trained dog coming to steal our secrets. Then he mumbled something about a parson and hung up."

Cartwright stared. "Our secrets? What secrets? The Osiris? How can a dog steal the Osiris?" He threw his head back and roared with laughter. "I hope the dog's got a pilot's licence!"

"I don't understand it, sir."

Cartwright laughed harder. "Maybe the parson's going to pray for good flying weather for the dog!"

Hayes smiled weakly. "Sir, should I report it to Security?"

The commanding officer was still laughing. "By all means. Snider's entitled to a good laugh too."

Hayes dialled Security.

*   *   *

"But, Chief, I'm just not ready yet!" shouted Lawrence Waghorn into the telephone. "I'm not even finished the outline! ... No, I can't give you an outline tomorrow ... At least a few more days ..." He hung up angrily.

The Chief is right, he reflected. Fine writer I am! I've finished a fraction of an outline, and all of that I got from some old lady who raves at the dinner table. Tonight she didn't say anything and I'm absolutely high and dry!

To try and put himself into the writing mood he looked over his outline as it stood. *The head agent is staying at the hotel with Z-2.* Hmmm. Parson's dog was stolen—why couldn't someone nab Z-2? Good idea!

Breathlessly he turned to the typewriter and began to type. With Z-2 gone, they'd probably send in Z-4 or Z-5, who are standing by. Hey, not bad. Not bad at all.

*   *   *

Richard Knight stood on his balcony and gazed out onto the moonlit grounds in deep thought. The Osiris operation was going to be difficult.

Not impossible, but very delicate. What on earth was he going to do about Cobber? The man was an idiot and a liability. But he was a pilot—a very good one, Knight had been told—and this assignment called for a pilot.

A sudden footstep below caught his attention and he leaned over the railing. His near-perfect night sight made out two figures on the lawn. His brows knit in perplexity—it was one of those Weston twins walking a black Labrador retriever. At two o'clock in the morning, it had to be the stolen dog belonging to the hotel manager. Certainly this was not the twin with the perpetually worried, conscientious look. Sidney, then, the one with the intense expression in his eyes. He was obviously harbouring Parson's dog. But why?

Knight's disciplined mind shifted back to the matter at hand. He must not let insignificant things monopolize his thoughts. There was too much at stake.

He watched until he was certain that Sidney and the dog had gone indoors. Then he stepped across to the balcony of Cobber's room and paused for a moment. Yes, this was definitely the right time to take a dry run with Cobber and sneak onto the air base. Cobber had to be familiarized with the base and with the technique of making undetected progress in the dark. It would be a while yet before they were engaged in the real thing, but it would be risky to hold the dress rehearsal too close to the actual day. Now, with the Osiris not yet ready for testing, the guard

would not be as heavy as it would be closer to the test day. So they would go tonight.

Silently he let himself in through the unlocked sliding doors. "Ready, Cobber?"

The pilot leaped out of an armchair. "Dick! Geez, you shouldn't sneak up on a guy like that!"

"Quiet. Follow me. And no talking."

Cobber opened his mouth to speak, but Knight froze him with a murderous look.

The two men slipped out of the hotel building, and keeping well into the shadows of the trees, moved towards the golf course. They crawled into the brush at the air base fence, and a few seconds later a small portion of the fence swung open like a gate. Knight and Cobber, their faces now darkened, emerged onto the base property. Knight took a quick survey of where the guards were, then turned to Cobber and whispered, "Stay close to me."

Cobber opened his mouth to speak, thought better of it and nodded. Carefully he followed Knight as the spy made cautious progress across the grounds. Knight's plan for this trial run was to show Cobber Hangar B, where the Osiris was housed. To get there they would stay close to the Officers' Quarters building, which would afford them cover.

The two men paused, crouched down under a row of windows.

Knight pointed. "Hangar B," he whispered.

Cobber nodded.

"Wait here for a minute," whispered Knight.

He began to edge down the row of windows, closer to the hangar.

Cobber's curiosity got the better of him. He stood up in front of the nearest window and peered inside. A look of joyful recognition spread over his face.

* * *

Wings Weinberg was dreaming. He was in the cockpit of the Osiris HE2 and everything was going wonderfully well. What an airplane! He was just coming in for a perfect landing after a flawless test when he woke up abruptly. Disoriented for an instant, he looked around the room, blinking. Suddenly his eyes fell on the window. A bolt of terror ripped through his body from head to toe, leaving him gasping. There was a face at the window—not just *a* face, *the* face. Bert Cobber!

Unable to find the breath to scream, Wings leaped out of bed, ran full-steam to the door, yanked it open and disappeared into the hall.

* * *

"I hope you've got a good reason for hauling me out of bed in the middle of the night, Sergeant," said Captain Snider, wearing pyjamas, housecoat, holster and gun.

"Well, sir," said the sergeant, "I figured you might want to be the first to know." He led Snider into the detention area.

There on a bench sat the pyjama-clad Wings Weinberg, chewing frantically on his fingernails.

Snider's jaw dropped. "Wings! What happened?"

The Legend looked up. "He's here," he said shakily. "Bert Cobber. I saw him."

Oh, no, thought Snider. Weinberg's gone off the deep end.

"There are no intruders on the base, sir," put in the sergeant. "I checked with all sentry points. Everything's quiet."

"That's fine, sergeant. Come on, Wings. I'll take you to your room."

"Should I notify Colonel Cartwright?" asked the sergeant.

"No!" exclaimed Snider. "I mean—I'll tell him in the morning. This incident is to be kept quiet, right, Sergeant?"

"Right, sir."

"Let's go, Wings."

*　*　*

"Cobber, you blithering fool!"

Knight and Cobber were back safely in Cobber's hotel room.

"I don't know what made me do it, Dick!"

"I don't know what made you do it either," said Knight coldly. "What on earth could make a man stupid enough to jeopardize so much for nothing?"

Cobber shrugged unhappily.

"And in direct disobedience of my orders. How dare you disobey me? The last person who did that regretted it—but only for a very short time. Do I make myself clear?"

"Yeah, mate. Really, I'm sorry. It won't happen again."

"Definitely not," said Knight. "Now go to sleep, and when you wake up tomorrow spend *all* your time studying the Osiris flight manual. And you might give a thought to being grateful that, for the moment, I need you. Goodnight."

*   *   *

Wings Weinberg sat on his bed and stared at his now tightly closed curtains. Snider hadn't believed him. He had said it was just a dream, a nightmare brought on by overwork. But it had seemed so real! That had been Bert Cobber's face leering at him from the window.

Suddenly he jumped up, ran to the window, paused nervously for an instant, then whipped the curtain back. Nothing. There was no one out there, only the night sentries at the fence in the distance.

I'm tired, thought Wings. I have to get some sleep. But how could he ignore this incident? Bert Cobber was in his world again.

Or was he? Maybe Snider was right. But just to be on the safe side . . .

Wings rushed to the closet, opened his trunk, rummaged around at the bottom and finally

came up with an old, old duffle bag. He had not looked inside this bag since his graduation from cadet training years ago. He shook it and choked as dirt puffed up into his face. With much effort, he opened the rusted zipper and fanned away the cloud of dust that rose from inside. Then he pulled out a small, dented picture frame and stared at it with loathing in his eyes. The photograph was of a younger, smiling Bert Cobber. On it Wings had written *Fly carefully* in orange crayon. He placed the picture on his bureau and reached back into the bag. Out came a small, battered night light with a broken base.

Wings surveyed the room. There was nowhere to plug it in. He donned his dressing gown and ventured out into the hall in search of an extension cord.

6

It's him again!

It was seven o'clock in the morning when the night light on the bureau beside the slumbering Wings Weinberg suddenly hurtled across the room and smashed against the door.

"*Owww!*" A loud cry of pain exploded from the hall.

Wings sat bolt upright, leaped out of bed and ran to the door, throwing it open.

There on the floor lay Colonel Cartwright, hopelessly entangled in the extension cord from the night light.

"What is this?" bawled the commanding officer.

"Uh—it's mine, sir. I needed to plug something in," explained Wings, "so I had to get an extension cord."

Captain Snider came running up, pistol in hand. "What happened? Colonel, are you all right?" He disentangled his C.O. from the long wire. "What's this doing here?" He looked at

Wings, who shrugged helplessly. Then his eyes fell on the broken light lying on the floor inside the room. He slammed the door quickly.

Colonel Cartwright struggled to his feet, and cradling his right arm, turned to Snider and Wings. "Well?" he demanded. "What was it?"

"Nothing, sir," said Snider. "Just an extension cord."

"I know it was an extension cord! I fell over it, didn't I? What was it attached to?" He threw open the door and stared dumbfounded at the night light. There was an awful silence for a moment. Then the bewildered C.O. pointed to the night light, turned and pointed to Weinberg, then looked at Snider questioningly.

Snider nodded unhappily.

Cartwright looked as though he had been struck. He cleared his throat carefully. "Weinberg, by any chance has anybody on this base said anything lately that might have embarrassed you?"

Wings looked surprised. "No, sir."

"That's what I was afraid of," said Cartwright, his face grey. "Snider, I want to see you in my office at once."

"But, sir—your arm—"

"There's nothing wrong with my arm," snapped Cartwright. "Colonel Weinberg, we'll see you later."

* * *

Oh, no, thought Sidney, staring through his magnifying glass at the sheet of carbon paper he had that morning taken from Lawrence Waghorn's wastebasket. He squinted. There was a blurry line of jumble, then: ... *temporarily set back by the abduction of Z-2, he sends immediately for Z-4. Though he remains in hiding, Z-5's training is increased in case he is pressed into service.* Sidney looked up. "Z-4 is coming!" he announced aloud to Blackie.

He didn't know what to do first. He had to write letters to keep the agencies informed on developments, but he had to find Z-4 before Waghorn could use him against the base. And the base had to be warned again. Not only that, but he was due for bellhop duty in the lobby.

Sidney affixed a small date sticker to the corner of the carbon and placed it in a file folder with the others. He rolled his bed away from the wall, removed the loose piece of panelling, swung open the wallboard and carefully stuffed the folder inside. Then, setting everything back to normal, he fixed his micro-camera into his belt buckle and set out for the lobby.

From behind the garbage can outside their door, Tom watched his brother's retreating back. What he had overheard had his senses reeling. Z-4 was coming—obviously a relative of that rotten Z-2. Was it in the letters? Or was it from another piece of carbon paper? And if so, where was Sidney getting those carbons?

Tom looked at his watch. He was late for bellhop duty. He started for the lobby via the stairs.

*   *   *

Tom rolled a luggage-laden cart towards the elevator, followed eagerly by a newly arrived family of four.

Sidney leaned on the reception desk, awaiting his first task.

"Straighten up, Tom," said Mr. Parson disapprovingly.

"Sorry, sir." Sidney stood at attention, then leaned forward and gawked as the front doors opened and a bearded man entered carrying a large portfolio and leading a well-groomed golden Labrador retriever.

It's Z-4! he thought excitedly. He had not expected the replacement dog to arrive so soon.

"Good morning, sir. Can I help you with your luggage?"

"Don't touch Vishnik's portfolio!" snapped the newcomer in an accent Sidney could not place. "This portfolio is Vishnik's life. Vishnik's existence centres on work in this portfolio." He smiled genially. "I am artist, yes?"

Parson rushed up to them. "What seems to be the matter here?"

"Nothing is matter. I am Vishnik. You expect maybe me?"

"Ah, yes, Mr. Vishnik," smiled the manager. "A pleasure to have you, sir. Your suite is ready."

"Uh—the dog, sir," put in Sidney. "Shall I take him out back to the kennel?"

"No!" thundered Vishnik. "Vishnik's dog stays with Vishnik!"

"It's quite all right, Tom," said Parson. "Mr. Vishnik has made special arrangements with the hotel. His dog will stay with him. Show him to Suite 106."

"Luggage is in car," said Vishnik, handing Sidney a set of keys. "Vishnik carries portfolio."

Carrying two suitcases and an enormous trunk full of art supplies, Sidney managed to struggle to Suite 106, leading Vishnik and his dog. As he received his tip, he fingered his belt buckle and snapped several pictures of the artist and the dog.

He went back to the lobby, his thoughts in a turmoil. Vishnik's dog was obviously Z-4, implying that Vishnik himself was involved. As an artist, he undoubtedly had a fine eye for detail and would make a superb spy. He would probably also draw up the final plans for action against the air base. Things were becoming very difficult for Sidney to keep on top of as the plot grew more and more complicated. It was clear, though, that the dog was the key and that he had to act immediately. The first question was how to kidnap Z-4.

A new group of guests was walking in the front door. As he went back to his work, Sidney made a mental note to warn the air base about Z-4 at the earliest opportunity, and to include Vishnik in his next dispatches to the various agencies.

*   *   *

"Do you mean to tell me," said Colonel Cartwright incredulously to Wings Weinberg, "that you completely blew your stack last night because you thought you saw some guy you knew nine years ago in cadet school?"

"It wasn't just 'some guy,' Colonel. It was Bert Cobber."

"According to Security, Weinberg, it was nobody. Right, Snider?"

Captain Snider nodded. "That was the report, sir."

"Okay," said Cartwright. "Now, Colonel Weinberg, there was no one at your window last night, least of all this Cobber person. Why don't we chalk all this up to fatigue or something and forget about it?"

"Yes, sir," said Wings.

"Good. Then I suggest that you go back to your quarters and study—"

There was a knock at the door and Corporal Hayes ventured timidly in. "Sorry for the interruption, sir."

Cartwright leaned back in his chair. "Well, Hayes, what can we do for you?"

"Sir, he called again."

"Who called again?"

"The person who called last night. At least, I think it was him. He was whispering this time too. It all happened so fast. He said that we should watch out because there's another dog—

84

there are lots of dogs. And then he said the parson was watching him and he hung up."

Cartwright was laughing again. "What kind of crank could it be? Did you tell him the Osiris is a one-dog aircraft?"

Hayes flushed. "He never mentioned the Osiris, sir. Nobody could know about it. It's top secret."

"You'd be amazed how much top-secret information gets around," said Snider grimly. "I don't like these phone calls."

"Don't worry about it, Snider," guffawed Cartwright. "How bad can it be with a parson mixed up in it?"

"Still," said Snider, "if these calls continue—"

"What's this about dogs?" asked Wings Weinberg. "There aren't going to be any dogs around here, are there?"

Cartwright sat up in alarm. "Don't tell me you're afraid of dogs!"

"Well, not really," began Wings, "but when I was a cadet my partner, Bert Cobber, kept this dog. He wasn't supposed to have a dog in the barracks, but he did anyway. It was a big Saint Bernard named Mushy. I've got teeth marks all over me from Mushy. Cobber used to smuggle him onto our plane and Mushy would attack me in flight. I learned to fly blind because that dog was always on my face." Wings sat in gloomy reflection. "Mushy was never house-broken. And he lived under *my* bed."

"Well, this can't be Mushy," decided Cartwright. "He'd be too old."

"Oh, Mushy was killed," replied Wings, "shot the time Cobber went nuts and accidentally strafed the base. But that's another story."

"What should I do, sir?" asked Hayes.

"If he calls again I want to be notified," said Snider. "It's probably a joke, but just in case—"

"Good idea," said Wings. "We don't want any dogs coming here." He stared moodily into space. "Mushy."

* * *

"Hey, Dick, did I ever tell you about Mushy?"

"No, you didn't," replied Knight, not looking up from a sketch map he was making of the Trillium security system, "and I'd just as soon pass."

"Mushy was the sweetest dog I ever saw. I kept him during my cadet days when I was with Wings. We had a lot of fun with Mushy."

"A boy and his dog," said Knight sarcastically. "How charming."

"Mushy and Wings got along so well. They were inseparable. Mushy even slept under Wings' bed."

"I am not interested, Cobber."

"They used to horse around all the time. On training flights Mushy would ride on Wings' head. It was great fun." His face turned tragic. "It's a shame Mushy died. He was shot, you know."

"I am devastated," said Knight. "And now, Cobber, spare me your reminiscences and make

proper use of your time by studying the manual of the Osiris HE2."

"Yeah, yeah, mate. I was going to anyway."

* * *

The Pine Grove recreation director, David Bishop, was working out on the rings. Since none of the guests had chosen to visit the gymnasium on this particular afternoon, there was nothing else to do. He might as well keep in shape.

As he jumped to the floor with athletic grace, he heard the sound of one person clapping and turned to see Lawrence Waghorn standing there.

"Oh, hi. I'm Dave Bishop. Can I help you at all? How about a workout?"

Waghorn smiled sadly. "No, thanks. Not me. I'm just moping around killing time while my career goes down the drain."

"You should never feel like that. Sometimes good old physical exercise is just what you need."

Waghorn shook his head. "I'm afraid good old physical exercise won't get my script written. I'm writing a spy story that takes place at a hotel."

"Oh, you mean a hotel like this one? That's a good idea. We've got an air base right next door."

"Yeah, that's what I'm working on. But the plot just doesn't seem to be clicking. Anyway, I won't bother you with my troubles."

"Maybe they've got some kind of secret airplane or something," suggested Bishop helpfully. "What else does an air base do?"

Waghorn brightened. "That's not a bad idea. My spies could be after their plane."

The ever-observant eye of Sidney Weston peered around the edge of the door frame. Another hotel employee, he thought, switching the micro-camera to his ring and snapping several pictures of the two men together. Bishop must be in on the plot. Sidney wasn't exactly sure what they were saying, but he had distinctly heard the words 'spies' and 'secret airplane.' So that was what Waghorn was after at Trillium! A secret aircraft!

"A secret airplane," repeated Waghorn. "Thanks a lot. Hmmm, what am I going to do with the dogs? Oh, well, thanks anyway." He started for the gymnasium door.

Unwilling to be caught eavesdropping, Sidney rushed inside a nearby utility closet.

"Hey!"

He found himself struggling with an unknown assailant. Sidney broke free of his attacker's grip and was preparing to defend life and country when there was a click and a light illuminated the closet.

"Mr. Kitzel!" exclaimed Sidney, helping the man to his feet. "What are you doing in here?"

"Hiding," whispered the elderly gentleman, catching his breath. "That Fuller woman is following me again! What does she want from my life?"

Sidney debated the wisdom of explaining about Miss Fuller's misguided spy hunt. He decided

against it. Kitzel sat at the same table as Waghorn. It would not do for the subject to come up. Waghorn was difficult enough to follow. If he went underground, pursuit would become hopeless.

Mr. Kitzel opened the closet door and peered both ways down the hall. "Ah, the coast is clear. I'm getting out of here while the getting is good." He dashed off.

Sidney remained in the closet to make sure there was absolutely no chance of being spotted by Waghorn. His mind was working furiously. Waghorn was after a plane, he thought, so the dogs could only be preliminary agents, used for scouting. It would take men to steal an airplane. Bishop was athletic and lithe and would be good at evading security. Was he also a pilot? Could Vishnik be a pilot? Was Waghorn himself the pilot? And Parson. Where did Parson fit in? He made the hotel hospitable to the spies and provided a cover for Z-2. Was that it? Or did he have a larger role as yet undiscovered? Sidney knew he would have to warn the air base yet again, and write some more letters. Earlier he had planted an electronic listening device in Waghorn's wastebasket. As soon as he was off duty he must listen to the tape that was being recorded. And he mustn't forget that there was still Z-4 to be dealt with.

The door flew open and another figure scrambled inside.

"Miss Fuller!"

"Oh, it's you," she panted. "Have you seen Mr. Kitzel? I do declare, he's hard to follow."

"Uh—Miss Fuller—uh—I really think you shouldn't—"

"He was headed in this direction when I last saw him," she insisted. "What's new on your end of the investigation?"

"The target is a secret airplane," whispered Sidney confidentially, "but I don't think Mr. Kitzel is—"

"What about your letters?" she interrupted. "Is help coming?"

"Not yet."

"Does the air base know about Mr. Kitzel?"

"Well, no."

"Well, warn them, for goodness' sake! That man is dangerous! Why, to look at him you wouldn't even know he's a pilot!"

Sidney goggled. "Mr. Kitzel is a pilot?"

"Well, of course he is. He must be, if he's going to steal an airplane."

"Oh," said Sidney, subdued. "But Mr. Kitzel is innocent."

"Yes, you'd think so to look at him, wouldn't you?"

Completely overwhelmed, Sidney sighed. "I guess so."

*   *   *

Dear Mr. Weston, read the letter from the Department of National Defence.

We must say it is very nice to hear from you again on the subject of our country's peril. We were afraid that things were too quiet since the frogman invasion off the coast of Newfoundland. We trust you have been well and ever on the alert, and we're eternally grateful to you for making our job so much easier and so much more fun.

We know nothing of your Mr. Waghorn, save the ordeal which no doubt awaits him. Perhaps he is a religious man and can find solace in prayer. We sincerely hope so, as he brings to mind the innocent Newfoundland fisherman, supposed mastermind of the frogman caper, who spent eight hours in a lobster trap while you caught up with the rest of his gang—Girl Scouts on an excursion.

Yours sincerely,
Mark

Hmmm, thought Sidney as Blackie wolfed down the filet portion of a large T-bone steak. National Defence hadn't heard of Waghorn either.

He glanced through the other letter, the one from the Prime Minister's office. The Prime Minister's secretary wrote that she had referred Sidney's letter to the OPP.

Hearing his brother outside the door, Sidney stashed the letters between his mattress and box spring and closed Blackie into the bathroom.

Tom entered the room. "Hi, Sidney. What's new?" He was hoping for a clue as to why his brother had been sneaking around the broom closet outside the gymnasium. Tom had been delivering towels to Dave Bishop when he had spotted the arrivals and departures of Sidney, Mr. Kitzel and Miss Fuller. Sinkingly aware that Sidney's investigation was in full swing, he had stayed around to watch.

"Nothing much," said Sidney airily.

"How's Z-2?"

"Shhh! Tom, don't ever let that name pass your lips. It's too dangerous."

"The only things dangerous about that mutt are his teeth!" snapped Tom. Frustrated with his subtle attempts to discover what Sidney was up to, he decided to revert to more direct methods. "So how's your friend, that Mr. Waghorn that you were taking pictures of earlier?"

"Sorry, but I'm on duty in the lounge," said Sidney, running out of the room.

Great, thought Tom, especially when he knew this was Sidney's night off. But it did prove one thing. Waghorn was still the target of Sidney's investigation—or at least one of the targets. Tom would have to check on his brother later. Right now he was due in the kitchen.

* * *

Table 19 had a new guest. Vishnik sat to the right of Bert Cobber, doing a portrait of the

92

finely chiselled features of Richard Knight in his mashed potatoes.

Cobber glanced over at Vishnik's plate. "Hey, Dick, look at this! It's you!"

The plate was passed around and admired by all. Knight had already noticed Vishnik's steady regard, and while relieved that the man was merely an artist, did not think much of having his face immortalized, in mashed potatoes or anything else.

Vishnik smiled broadly at Knight. "You are beautiful, yes? Vishnik will paint you."

"I am honoured," said Knight with a slight bow, "but I fear I must decline. I am superstitious about things like that."

Edna Fuller spoke up. "Why don't you paint Mr. Kitzel here?"

The artist bristled. "He"—indicating Knight— "is like Greek god; he"—pointing at Kitzel—"is like toad with full mouth."

Mr. Kitzel looked up. "Please pass the sour cream."

"So Vishnik will paint Greek god," decided the artist.

"No, thank you," said Richard Knight suavely.

"Well, Mr. Kitzel," said Miss Fuller, "you've certainly been all over the hotel lately. You might say you've been just—*flying* around."

Knight glanced at Fuller oddly. Kitzel did not look up from his cheese blintzes. He had decided to pretend his hearing aid was malfunctioning.

Undaunted, Miss Fuller smiled brilliantly at

Vishnik. "We play a little spy game here at Table 19. We're trying to decide how a spy could break into the air base up the road and steal something —oh, let's say a secret airplane."

Knight upset his water glass in order to draw attention from Cobber's dismay. The pilot was choking uncontrollably into his napkin.

Waghorn stared at Miss Fuller in amazement. The woman had come up with the same idea he had. Was it a coincidence, or was she a spy from another television network? After all, he had already typed the latest instalment to his outline. Could she have gone through his garbage and read it off his carbons? He had always thought it strange that, although his suite was in the middle of the hall, his garbage was collected first. It all fit! She fed him the first part of a story so he could finish it for her. Well, that was it! She was not going to get anything more from him!

"Why an airplane?" asked Bert Cobber in a strangled voice.

"What would you expect to find at an air base?" asked the cool voice of Richard Knight. "A ship?"

"But, Dick—"

"Isn't it a lovely game?" beamed Edna Fuller. "The dogs do the preliminary work—we've already established that. And then some pilot comes in, gets into the plane and flies off with it."

Cobber's choking worsened.

Vishnik looked from Miss Fuller to Knight. "The woman is crazy, yes?"

94

Knight shrugged expressively and Vishnik turned back to his dinner.

Lawrence Waghorn set his jaw and stared defiantly at Miss Fuller.

She said, "What do *you* think, Mr. Kitzel?"

"Delicious," he mumbled, his mouth full.

* * *

As the guests ate their dinner, Sidney Weston crouched outside the window of Vishnik's first-floor suite. Using equipment he had purchased "for a song" from a mail-in offer in *Clue* magazine, he had no trouble removing the screen. Inside, the dog trotted to the middle of the bedroom, where he eyed the boy suspiciously.

Slowly Sidney raised the window. The dog growled.

From his pocket Sidney produced a large filet mignon on a string. He tossed the steak in through the open window. As the dog jumped for it, Sidney pulled sharply on the string. The dog followed. When the steak flew out through the window, so did the dog. Sidney took off on the run for the entrance to the staff wing, the dog following in hot pursuit of his filet mignon.

"Here you go, Z-4," said Sidney as he let himself and Vishnik's dog into his room. "Here's your new home."

Blackie ran up to greet them. Both dogs licked Sidney's face lovingly.

*　*　*

"You! Parson!" stormed the angry artist. "Vishnik's dog is no longer with Vishnik! Vishnik's dog is missing! Where is Vishnik's dog?"

Tom Weston, cleaning ashtrays in the lobby, felt his heart lurch. Sidney. Oh, no!

"Oh, dear," said Parson, "another dog theft. I'll call hotel security."

"Hotel will find Vishnik's dog, yes?"

"We'll do everything we can," promised the manager. "My own dog went missing a couple of days ago, so I know what you're going through."

"If you do not find Vishnik's dog," promised the artist, "Vishnik will take this entire hotel apart brick by brick and throw it in the swimming pool—until Vishnik's dog is back with Vishnik!"

Tom left the lobby hurriedly and rushed to his room in the staff wing. He threw open the door to see Sidney sitting deep in thought between Blackie and Vishnik's golden retriever, a hand absently patting each.

Tom's heart sank. "Z-4, I presume?"

There were two identical barks of rage as both dogs tore away from Sidney after Tom. Once again Tom climbed the bookshelves and sat cowering, staring down at the two canines.

"Come on down, Tom," chided Sidney. "There's nothing to be afraid of. These two dogs are as harmless as pussycats. That's something I've figured out about the Z series. These dogs are

96

okay until they're under orders. Then they're deadly. What I want to know is how you knew this was Z-4."

"Who else would you kidnap?" asked Tom sarcastically. "Lassie?"

"Ah, but why not Z-1 or Z-3?"

"You talked in your sleep again," lied Tom glibly. "Sidney, we are not keeping these dogs another minute!"

"We have to. Come down here. I want to talk to you."

"Call off your two monsters first."

Sidney put the two dogs in the bathroom and Tom climbed down. "All right, come clean. What's been going on?"

Sidney cleared his throat. "There's a plot under way that involves the fate of the western world."

Tom stared at him. "So?"

"These two dogs are involved in it." There, he thought. Now that Tom could feel he was being levelled with, perhaps he would stop being so suspicious and leave Sidney alone to get on with his investigation.

"And?" prompted Tom. He awaited further explanation—the carbons, the listening devices, Lawrence Waghorn, the mysterious eighty dollar purchase.

"That's it," said Sidney. "That's what's going on."

Tom just stood there, struck dumb. Sidney hadn't told him anything, and obviously he had no intention of doing so.

Maybe Tom would like to be part of things, thought Sidney generously. "Now I want to ask you to do me a favour, Tom." He held out a stack of letters. "Would you please mail these for me?"

"Certainly." Tom grabbed the letters, ran out of the room, took the elevator to the lobby and tossed the letters into the nearest waste receptacle. Then, cheerful despite his frustration, he returned to polishing ashtrays.

Edna Fuller, a crumpled piece of tissue in her hand, leaned over the wastebasket. "Oh, my goodness!" There were letters there addressed to important government agencies. She checked the return address—S. Weston. Sidney's letters had somehow found their way into the garbage. They must be mailed. They contained important information about Mr. Kitzel. She scooped the stack of letters out of the garbage can and dutifully dropped them into the mail slot.

Watching from across the room, Tom slapped his forehead in despair.

Mr. Parson happened along. "Been writing some letters, Miss Fuller?" he asked in a friendly tone.

"Who wants to know?" she replied belligerently. This was classified information—none of his business.

Parson stiffened with shock. "I—I see. Well, have a nice evening."

* * *

Lawrence Waghorn entered his room, still raging. He had thought that an after-dinner drink might calm him down, but even four hadn't done the trick. That Fuller woman! How dare she spy on him.

What a stupid business he had gone into—television writing. Writing was an art and television was big business. The two just didn't mix. How could he be creative when there was danger of someone stealing his work?

In frustration, he kicked his wastebasket. There was a rattling sound, and a small black object bounced out and landed on the carpet at his feet. Waghorn picked it up and turned it over in his hand, his face tense with shock. He had written enough spy and detective stories to know what this was—an electronic listening device. That Fuller woman had bugged his room!

Furiously, he held the bug close to his mouth and bellowed, "You're not going to get anything from me! You hear that? *Nothing!*"

He ran out onto his balcony, wound up like a major-league pitcher and heaved the bug as far as he could.

"There!" he said with satisfaction. "That must have gone all the way to the seventh tee! Let her listen to that!"

* * *

"Captain Snider!" hissed Corporal Hayes urgently. "Take the other line! It's him again!"

Snider picked up the extension in time to hear a voice speaking in a muffled whisper say, "... the second dog is under control, but you have to expect a third. Bishop is in on it as well as Parson, and Vishnik too is involved. I'm not sure yet who the pilot is. There's Parson. I've got to go." There was a click and then a dial tone.

Hayes and Snider looked at each other in bewilderment.

"Well," said Colonel Cartwright in great good humour, "don't leave me out of it. What was it this time?"

"The parson again," said Hayes, "and more about dogs."

"And a bishop too," added Snider.

"A bishop?" repeated Cartwright jovially. "Any cardinals?"

"Then he mentioned something about vishnik," said Hayes. "Or that's what it sounded like."

"Vishnik?" said Snider. "I've had vishnik. It's a cherry brandy with a kick like a mule."

"I know!" laughed Cartwright. "The parson and the bishop have gotten into the vishnik and they're making crank calls!"

"He also mentioned a pilot," said Snider, dead serious. "That could mean someone knows about the Osiris. I'm going to set up equipment and try to trace the next call."

Cartwright laughed harder. "You're just sore, Snider, because the parson and the bishop won't give you any of that vishnik."

Snider smiled grimly. "Colonel, this may be more serious than we think."

"Hah! Snider, you're serious about the wrong thing. Here you are worrying over a couple of crank calls when the great Wings Weinberg is going insane on my base! How would you like to be C.O. of the base where the brilliant career of the world's greatest test pilot comes to an end because he flips his lid? How'd you like to be a corporal again? No offence, Hayes."

Snider shuffled uncomfortably. "Wings will be all right, Colonel."

"He'd better be," snapped Cartwright. "I'm not going to have that kind of thing on *my* record. So from now on, Snider, I want you to babysit Weinberg. Spend your every waking hour with him and somehow or other get him through that test flight and off my base!"

"But, sir," Snider protested, "I'm the security officer."

"Well, there you are, then. Make him feel secure. Just get him through that test. Is that clear?"

"Yes, sir."

*　*　*

Richard Knight leaned over his balcony watching the lone figure of Sidney Weston walking two large dogs—one Parson's Blackie, the other a golden retriever undoubtedly belonging to the artist Vishnik.

Was this boy acting out Miss Fuller's spy game? It seemed so. Yet he did not seem to be after Kitzel. Knight remembered the drinking

glass Sidney had so carefully spirited away with waxed paper. If the boy were after anyone, it was Lawrence Waghorn. Come to think of it, earlier on, Waghorn had had a habit of jumping up and running away every time Table 19 played the spy game.

Knight decided it was time he did some investigating on some of his table mates. Sidney Weston might bear inspection too.

7

Temporarily out of commission

Sidney walked up to the hot-tray that the chef was preparing for Mr. Parson's breakfast. It was the manager's custom to take all his meals in his private suite. From his sleeve Sidney palmed a small plastic bottle with an eyedropper. As he studied the contents of the tray, his eyes fell on a tall glass of orange juice. With great stealth and dexterity, he emptied two drops of clear liquid from the dropper into the juice.

While Sidney was selecting his own breakfast, he spied Tom picking up the hot-tray for delivery to the hotel manager and tossed over his shoulder, "You be careful with that. Make sure it gets where it's going." Tom cast him a suspicious glance as he walked out into the hall.

Sidney picked up his tray and sat down beside David Bishop. As always, the athlete was starting the day off right with a hearty breakfast—six fried eggs, a stack of pancakes, several sausages, toast and a tall glass of milk. Bishop's milk glass was empty.

With much effort Sidney downed his own milk in three enormous gulps and sighed loudly to attract Bishop's attention.

"That was delicious! I'm going to get some more. Want some?"

"Thanks." The recreation director handed Sidney his glass. "As I always say, 'milk is the only drink there is.'"

"Right." Sidney returned to the counter, filled both glasses with milk and slipped two drops of the liquid from the bottle into Bishop's drink.

He watched as Bishop gulped down his milk with great relish. Two down and two to go, he thought. Now, how was he going to get to Waghorn and Vishnik?

Tom's voice disturbed his thoughts. "Sidney, I didn't like the sound of that 'make sure it gets where it's going.' What did you do to Parson's breakfast?"

"Oh," said Sidney airily, "nothing much."

"Look, I saw you. I know you did something. What was it?"

"It's not necessary for you to know." Sidney jumped up and ran over to the Table 19 waiter, who had a trayful of orange juice. "I'll serve that for you."

"Thanks."

Tom watched in horror as his brother stealthily slipped something from an eyedropper into the two end glasses and began to carry the tray out into the dining room. From the doorway he carefully took note of who received which glass.

The treated glasses went to Waghorn and Vishnik.

Vishnik raised his glass. Out of the kitchen burst Tom, moving at top speed, his red jacket just a blur. He tore down the centre of the dining room and snatched the glass of orange juice from Vishnik's lips.

"You don't want to drink that! We have grapefruit juice! It's better for you!"

Seeing Waghorn make a motion towards his glass, Tom lunged across the table, overturning the glass and spilling orange juice on the white tablecloth and Waghorn's lap.

Waghorn backed away in his chair as the juice spilled off the table onto the floor.

"What the—"

"I'll send for a new tablecloth," cried Tom, and rushed back into the kitchen.

"Are you guys crazy?" bellowed the waiter. "Now I've got to set up the table again!"

"Tom, why did you do that?" asked Sidney angrily. "Don't interfere!"

"I had to! You can't just go around poisoning people!"

"It wasn't poison. It was a fast-acting high-powered laxative. By lunch time they would all have been out of commission."

"You can't do that!"

Sidney looked puzzled. "Why not?"

"If the guests start getting sick, they're going to investigate the kitchen to see what caused it," raged Tom. "There'll be a whole big ruckus!"

Sidney looked at him. "Good thinking. If too much attention is brought to this, I won't be able to make proper use of the time I buy."

"What proper use? What are you up to now?"

"Oh, nothing. Anyway, thanks for your quick thinking."

"I was just trying to save our jobs."

"Yeah, well, cover for me for a few minutes, will you? I'm going to the meat locker to get some food for the dogs."

"You'll be able to let them go soon," said Tom sarcastically. "The way you've been feeding them, before too long they'll be too *fat* to threaten the western world!"

* * *

Bundled in a pressure suit, Wings Weinberg was shut into the Osiris simulator where he would be tested under conditions similar to those he would encounter on his test flight.

"How has he been?" asked Cartwright anxiously.

"Well, I guess he's okay," replied Captain Snider. "He's a little quiet, but he seems to have settled down. I think he'll come through."

"He'd *better* come through! If he can't score over seventy on this thing they won't let him fly the Osiris. And then, Snider, the two of us might as well open a shoe store, because we're finished in the service."

"Just give him a chance, Colonel."

"Oh, I'll give him a chance," said the commanding officer. "I want to see his scores on the simulator. Let's see if that creampuff can fly at all, let alone like the best test pilot in the world!" He began to walk back towards his office. "Send Hayes the results as soon as they're available. And pray!"

* * *

After the first half of morning duty, Sidney and Tom met in front of their room. Tom had been waiting.

"I don't dare go in there without you," he said, inserting his key in the lock. "You forgot to shut the dogs in the bathroom this morning and they're loose in the room."

Sidney was visibly upset. In his hand he held a plastic bag filled with ashes. Waghorn was burning his used carbon paper. That meant he knew that whoever was onto him had been reading his carbons.

"What's that?" asked Tom, pointing to the ashes. "The last remains of Parson after a taste of your laxative?"

Sidney was too overcome by his troubles to reply. He reached into his pocket and pulled out two letters he had picked up at the mail desk.

The twins walked into the room. Blackie and Vishnik's dog trotted over to Sidney lovingly, casting unfriendly glances at Tom.

"Anyway, your clothes arrived today." Tom in-

dicated a large bundle on the floor just inside the door. "I just tossed it in and ran. I didn't have the guts to face the two charter members of the Z-series. I see you got some more mail." He peered over Sidney's shoulder. "Norad—say, what does that stand for?"

"North American Air Defence," said Sidney. He sat down at his desk and opened the letter.

Dear Sidney,

It's great to hear from you again. All the guys send regards. It gets pretty boring around here from time to time, so when your letter arrived, it made our day. After all, it's been almost three months since you sent us the intricate map of every weather balloon over the North American continent with instructions to shoot them all down as they were obviously spy ships from a foreign power. It may please you to know that petty cash paid for framing the map, and we have hung it over the filing cabinet that contains your letters.

We assure you that we know of no spy plot against Trillium Base, and we have never heard of your Mr. Waghorn. We strongly suggest that you butt out, as you may find that the military does not have quite the sense of humour of the Weather Bureau. And they carry guns. Perhaps you can find enough to occupy yourself in that

Waghorn fellow, even though his photo
shows him to be a rather innocuous-looking
chap.

Please write and let us know how it all
turns out.
Regards,
Steve

"Well, what does this one say," asked Tom in
disgust.

"Nothing," said Sidney casually. "Steve is just
telling me routine stuff."

"Who's Steve?"

"General McAllister."

"You're on a first-name basis with a *general?"*

"Well, yes. Quite a while ago he started asking
to see all my letters personally. He answers them
all himself now."

Tom shook his head. No wonder the western
world was in peril all the time when Norad generals had nothing better to do than write letters to
idiots. "I'm going to take a shower," he announced. He headed for the bathroom.

Sidney frowned. The mail was so slow. Here
was Norad answering an old letter when there
were others on the way telling them about the
dogs, Parson, Bishop and Vishnik—and more photographs too. Steve wanted him to stay away
from the air base. The plane must be really top
secret, he supposed, and he didn't have security
clearance yet.

He opened the second letter. It read:

Dear Mr. Weston,

We received the letter referred to us by the Prime Minister's office. We did not read it. We threw it out.
Yours truly,
Ontario Provincial Police

With the shower running full blast in the bathroom, Sidney rushed to his table lamp, removed the shade and rewound the tape that had been recorded yesterday. He set it on play and began to listen.

There were the normal noises of Waghorn in his room, and very little else. He played the tape at high speed until he heard something of interest. Then he returned it to normal speed and listened.

After a loud crash and a low bumping sound, the loud voice of an enraged Lawrence Waghorn shouted, "You're not going to get anything from me! You hear that? *Nothing!*"

Then came frantic footsteps and a strange whistling sound, followed by a tremendous thud and finally silence.

Sidney switched off the tape and checked on what his bug was picking up now. There were birds and crickets chirping, and the buzzing sound of insects. In the distance he could hear people talking. He thought he heard someone yell "Fore!" Obviously this bug was not going to be of any further use to him. He set the lamp back to normal.

Well, one thing was certain—Waghorn was starting to be a little more careful. In that case, Sidney would have to be more careful as well. For one thing, it was now time to implement his newest purchase.

With the shower still running at full, Sidney walked over to the long bureau which held the TV set. He pushed the set aside, and by lifting twin handles, pulled out his eighty dollar purchase. Attached to the machine was a small booklet, *How to Use Your Intrepid Electronic Deluxe Homing System.*

On the first page Sidney read: *This system will track the ten homing pins supplied and distinguish between them at your specified range. Merely place a pin on the person or thing you intend to track and switch the scope to "on." The screen will show the exact location of each pin.*

He leafed through the rest of the booklet. This was fantastic! He could calibrate the range for his personal needs and mark the air base fence on the screen. Why, he could even set the built-in alarm to go off if one of the homing pins crossed over that fence. And the pins themselves were so small. There was no way his suspects would notice them.

Just to see what it would look like, he flicked the switch to "on." A high-pitched, pulsating beep began, and the receiver plate on top began to rotate. The screen showed ten dots right at the centre.

It works! thought Sidney triumphantly.

He heard Tom turn off the water and push the shower curtain aside. Quickly he pushed his homing device back into hiding and replaced the television set on top. He put the small box of homing pins in his pocket.

*　*　*

"I'll not be down to lunch, Cobber," announced Richard Knight. "I hope I can trust you to keep your mouth shut and behave yourself."

"Aw, you know me, Dick."

"Yes, I do," replied Knight, "but I am forced to trust you anyway."

"What are you going to be doing?" asked Cobber. "Can I go with you?"

"No."

"Why not, mate? You always leave me out of everything!"

"Cobber, this is no concern of yours. All I want you to do is go to the lunch table and cover for my absence."

"Oh, all right, mate. I'll say you're too sick to eat."

"You will say nothing," Knight instructed severely, "unless someone asks, in which case you will inform him that I've gone to town for a while."

"Aw, mate, why can't I go with you? It's boring here! Come on, where are we going?"

Knight's face darkened. "You are becoming a

nuisance, Cobber. The last person who became a nuisance had a most regrettable accident."

"Yeah, yeah, mate. All right. Anything you say."

* * *

"I have Lieutenant-Colonel Weinberg's simulator test results, sir," announced Corporal Hayes.

Cartwright had been sitting on the edge of his chair all morning. "Okay," he said, bracing himself. "How did he do?"

Hayes' brow furrowed. "It's kind of confusing, sir. Lieutenant Jones said that he displayed all the symptoms of emotional instability and extreme lack of sleep. He also seemed to be really nervous because his heart beat went way above normal."

"Oh, no!" cried Cartwright. "It's happened!" He slumped his head down onto his crossed arms. "I'm finished! They'll never let him fly now! The Norad people will get here and there'll be no test —just the shuddering hulk that used to be the legendary Wings Weinberg! Why me?"

"Well, you see, sir," said Hayes, "there's also his flying accuracy." He frowned. "That's the confusing part. His flying accuracy score was 99.4 percent."

Cartwright's head jerked up. "What? Impossible! No one can fly like that!"

"That's what Lieutenant Jones said, sir, but Colonel Weinberg did it. Take-off: 99.7; man-

oeuvres: 99.3; landing: 99.2. It's the highest score in history, sir."

A broad grin replaced Cartwright's look of dismay. "Amazing! Good old Wings! What a pilot! Get him in here, Hayes. I want to congratulate him personally."

"Uh—that's impossible, sir."

"Why?"

"Lieutenant-Colonel Weinberg is taking a nap, sir. He hasn't been sleeping well lately."

"Oh." Cartwright gritted his teeth. After all, Weinberg had scored 99.4 on the simulator. So what if he was a little nervous? We all have our idiosyncrasies.

*　*　*

Richard Knight let himself into his room and sat down to evaluate his findings about his table mates.

Mr. Kitzel. A cursory glance at the man's room had shown him to be exactly what he appeared to be.

Vishnik. He too was harmless—a very talented and eccentric artist on a painting trip. The only thing out of the ordinary was the theft of his dog.

Edna Fuller. She was a woman on vacation who, somehow, had decided that Kitzel was a super-spy, and who was making the poor man's life miserable.

Lawrence K. Waghorn. The man appeared to be some sort of scriptwriter. For some reason, the

story he was working on was about spies staying at a hotel and plotting to steal an airplane from a nearby military base. In addition to this unpleasant coincidence, Waghorn's story matched exactly Edna Fuller's spy game. This meant that Waghorn was cribbing from Fuller. However, it was just possible that the cribbing was working the other way round. Waghorn seemed paranoid about his story being stolen. His used carbons were burnt in his basket, and he had hidden his manuscript in a plastic bag inside the toilet tank in his bathroom. He was fearful of espionage either by Fuller or by—whom?

Sidney Weston. Knight had not had the opportunity to search Sidney's room, but it seemed apparent that the boy was the catalyst for the whole spy idea. Fuller was close to the boy, so he was probably responsible for putting spies on her mind. She must have decided on Kitzel on her own, as Sidney's suspicions were obviously centred on Waghorn. Apparently Sidney was following Waghorn's story, not recognizing it for fiction, and that explained why he had kidnapped the two dogs.

Knight sat quietly digesting this information. The situation, while alarming at times, did not seem to pose any threats to himself and Cobber. The only person who might conceivably become a nuisance was the Weston boy, but even he was only a kid playing detective. Briefly Knight toyed with the idea of attempting to have Sidney fired, but decided against it. He did not wish to bring

attention to himself or Cobber, and the confusion over exactly which Weston was being fired was certain to cause a stir. Still, the boy would bear watching. As for the Waghorn script, he and Cobber would have the Osiris long before the story could ever be released for motion pictures or television.

The situation, then, was reasonably safe. A little extra caution around Sidney Weston was all that was required. His major liability remained Cobber.

He set his mind to the problem of getting Cobber undetected from his hotel room to the cockpit of the Osiris HE2.

* * *

Corporal Hayes picked up the receiver, and hearing the voice, signalled to Snider with his free arm. The security chief quickly switched on the tracing equipment.

"Keep him on as long as you can," he whispered.

Hayes listened for a while, then, "Could you please repeat that, sir, a little louder this time? I'm having trouble hearing you." There was another pause, then, "Here, sir, I'll put you through to Captain Snider."

Snider took the line and the caller started over again. Snider held him up as much as possible by punctuating the conversation with "pardon me's" and "would you repeat that's." Finally he said,

116

"Sir, perhaps you'd better speak to the commanding officer."

Cartwright eagerly took the line, grinning broadly. He had never really taken these calls seriously and was anxious to hear the crackpot on the other end.

"Colonel Cartwright speaking. Hi, there—You don't say!...You've done away with the parson and the bishop? Good heavens, man, you can't just kill two clergymen!...Oh, it's only temporary...*Laxatives?*" Cartwright burst into laughter. When he got himself under control, he continued, "So how are the dogs?...Burnt carbon paper? How interesting...The *what*-horn?... What is a wag-horn? Does it have anything to do with the dogs? Never mind. When are we going to get together over some of that vishnik?...Oh, I quite understand. Goodbye." He hung up. "Well, Snider? Did you get it?"

The captain was labouring over his equipment. "I think so, sir."

Cartwright's face was flushed with pleasure. "I sure hope he calls back sometime. What a nut!"

"Yep," Snider confirmed, "I got it."

* * *

Captain Snider marched through the heavy glass doors into the lobby of the Pine Grove Resort Hotel. The number had been traced to one of the lobby phones there.

In his mind he went over Cartwright's instruc-

tions. "Keep a low profile," the commanding officer had said. "We don't want to call attention to the base with the Osiris around. Make it sound routine. You're just a neighbour dropping in to see how things are."

Snider stepped up to the desk clerk. "Excuse me. Could I please speak with the manager?"

"I'm sorry, Captain," replied the clerk. "The manager is not available. May I be of some assistance? I'm acting as manager for today."

Snider nodded. "Is there someplace we can talk privately? It won't take long."

"Certainly, sir. Follow me. Weston, take over the desk."

Without taking his eyes from the uniformed security chief, Sidney slipped behind the counter.

A white-faced Bert Cobber peered above the newspaper he had been reading as the two men disappeared into the manager's office.

* * *

Cobber burst unannounced into Richard Knight's room. Knight was sitting in an armchair, deep in thought.

"It is customary to knock," he said.

"Dick!" cried Cobber, barely coherent. "Dick, we're in big trouble! There was some army officer down there talking to the desk clerk! They're onto us! We've got to clear out of here!"

"I saw him arrive, Cobber. His name is Snider and he is a captain—the security chief of Trillium Base."

118

"But, Dick! He got a staff list and a guest list! He's going to find us on it!"

"I think not," said Knight with quiet confidence. "You see, just after we checked in I took the liberty of erasing any record of our rooms from the computer. Since these rooms do not exist, it follows that we cannot possibly be occupying them, and thus are not on the guest list."

Cobber was unimpressed. "Won't they catch the mistake?"

"Eventually," Knight conceded, "but not for some months. I assure you we are quite safe here."

"But, Dick, what was he doing here, that captain? He made them shut down all the lobby phones until further notice!"

Knight raised an eyebrow. "Indeed."

"Yeah! Mate, we've got to blow this joint!"

"We shan't be leaving, Cobber, until our business is completed."

"Well, maybe you want to stay, but I'm cutting out! I'm not going to jail!"

Knight looked threateningly up at him. "The last person who ran out on me met with some difficulties involving a cement truck."

Cobber went white again. "Don't get the wrong impression, mate. I'm with you all the way."

"I'm very happy to hear that," said Knight dryly. "Meanwhile, Cobber, do not concern yourself with these matters. Leave them to me. Now, have you memorized the Osiris flight manual yet?"

"Well—uh—actually—"

"Do so *now*," Knight ordered. "When you are finished with the photographs, they will be burned. Is that clear?"

"Yeah, mate, you've got it."

* * *

This was amazing, thought Sidney. It was all getting to be too much for him. Today a captain from the air base had arrived, asking for the manager. Sidney had been about to approach him when it had occurred to him that if this guy wanted to see Parson he could be in with Waghorn's organization. Sidney was glad he had held back. On the officer's way out he had stopped to talk to Vishnik on the lawn!

Vishnik was another enigma. The commanding officer of Trillium Base had distinctly mentioned Vishnik. Could Vishnik be bigger in the organization than Sidney had thought? And why would Vishnik sit out on the front lawn all day and paint? He couldn't see the air base from there. Maybe he'd been waiting to make contact with the soldier. That was it! There was an inside man at Trillium! Why, he'd even got them to shut down the lobby phones, the ones Sidney had been using to warn the base!

Hmmm, he thought, he would have to write another batch of letters and find another phone. And tomorrow he would definitely have to plant those homing pins. It was becoming crucial to know the whereabouts of the conspirators at all times.

*   *   *

"Honestly, chief, just a few more days now," promised Lawrence Waghorn over his phone. "I've finished the outline and I'm working on the script... Well, I'd have it done by now but there was a hold-up. There's this woman, Fuller is her name, and she's a spy from another network. I've had to take a lot of precautions to make sure she doesn't steal my story... Yes, I'm sure... Okay, chief, I'll finish it as quickly as possible. Good-bye."

He hung up the phone, in a good mood for a change. The chief was still rushing him, but the chief always did that. In the end he would have the time he needed. And his story was going well.

*   *   *

Richard Knight sat on his balcony puzzling over the new situation. Things were obviously not as under control as he had led Cobber to believe, but that had been necessary. Cobber was enough of a liability without having him scared.

Why had Snider visited the hotel? What did he want with a list of the staff and guests? Why disconnect the lobby phones? It was impossible for the base to know about himself and Cobber. There seemed no explanation for Snider's visit.

There were rustling noises below and Knight looked down. It was Sidney Weston again, taking the dogs for a walk under cover of the late-night darkness.

Of course! Sidney Weston! If the boy believed that the base was in danger, he might have phoned a warning to them. And Snider had traced the call to the hotel.

Knight relaxed a little. Sidney Weston, with his immensely distorted view of the situation, could not help but confuse the air base. Sidney wasn't threatening the base; he was attempting to help them. But because of the boy's outrageous story and his cloak-and-dagger manner, Snider regarded *Sidney* as the threat.

It seemed that Sidney Weston would not hinder Knight's business. He might even prove to be an asset, leading base security on a wild goose chase.

"Certainly, *sir!*" Simcha had never heard of the hotel, but he decided to take Snider's word that it was there.

"The situation is this. An unidentified person has been telephoning us from the hotel, claiming that the base is in some kind of danger. In these calls he's been mentioning the names Parson, Bishop, Vishnik and Waghorn. Have you got that?"

"Right, *sir!*"

"Okay. Now, as you can see, we have very little to go on, but each one of these names corresponds to a person on the guest list or the staff list." Snider handed the lieutenant a copy of each. "They're underlined in red. Also, there are two stolen dogs that we'd like to know about. Is this all clear?"

"Crystal clear, *sir!*"

"Good, Simcha. Here is your assignment. We're sending you to the hotel as a guest. You'll use your own name—only obviously you won't call yourself 'lieutenant.' Keep an eye on things over there and report back what you find. Okay?"

Simcha did not have the slightest idea what Captain Snider was talking about. All he knew was that he was being sent to a hotel. Was he getting a furlough? No, he seemed to be on assignment. What was the purpose of this list with the names underlined in red? What did the captain want?

Simcha got to his feet and snapped to attention. "I understand perfectly, *sir!*"

"Good," Cartwright cut in. "One last thing, lieutenant. As we all know, the Osiris is top secret. Don't do anything to bring attention to yourself or the base. The situation is very, very delicate. Got it?"

Simcha looked at his commanding officer. He did not understand him either, so he said briskly, "I recognize how delicate the situation is, *sir!*"

"Fine. You leave immediately. Good luck."

When the young lieutenant was gone, Cartwright turned to Snider and said, "Fine young man, that. All military. Reminds me of Weinberg before he went nuts with this Cobber thing. And by the way, where *is* Weinberg?"

"He's in his room, sir. Resting."

"I think that boy rests too much. That's his problem. Take him into town today, Snider. Get him off the base. The change'll do him good."

"Yes, sir."

* * *

Mr. Kitzel lay troubled in his bed. This whole wonderful holiday was being ruined by that awful Fuller woman. Everything would be fine if she would stop following him around and bothering him. She obviously wasn't in love with him. What did she want?

"*Oh, no!*" He sat bolt upright in a cold sweat as a sudden thought struck him. What if Edna Fuller was an income tax investigator? Maybe she knew that he had exaggerated a little on last

year's tax return. Could she suspect that Sarah Kitzel was not a dependent daughter but, in fact, a cat? Was Revenue Canada after him?

Mr. Kitzel glanced at the clock. He had missed breakfast, but at lunch he would have to find some way to convince Miss Fuller that he was an honest taxpayer.

* * *

Tom made a safe entry into his room that morning as the two dogs were occupied with several portions of ground beef. Sidney was seated at the desk, furiously licking stamps and envelopes.

"A whole bunch of letters arrived today," called Tom. "Seven of them. Here." He tossed them onto the desk. He had finally decided that there was no point in interfering with Sidney's mail, especially when it was probably going to get where it was going anyway.

"Great!" Sidney pushed away the outgoing mail and devoted his attention to the incoming. The first letter he opened was from the RCMP.

Dear Mr. Weston,

Wow. We were beginning to think you had lost your flair, but we were wrong. You're back in full form. Some of us say this is your best effort yet; I especially like the part about the dogs.

We know nothing about Walter Parson or David Bishop. As for Mr. Vishnik, we

think his work is excellent, especially the surreal "Cosmos" hanging in the Ontario Art Gallery.

We are still not assigning any men to either you or Trillium Base. We suggest you try the dogcatcher's office. Please keep us posted. I've got five bucks on Mr. Parson in the conservatory with the lead pipe.
Best wishes,
Bruce

Sidney read through his other letters. Mark, from the Department of National Defence, sent his regards to Z-2, Z-4 and Vishnik, while Connie from NATO simply said hello. Steve, the Norad general, once again urged Sidney to stay away from the base, but did send his regards to everyone and mentioned that if Z-5 made his appearance within the next three days, he would win fifty dollars. Z-5 was a longshot at five to one, Steve explained, and he, as a general, should rightfully win. Around Norad the favourite was for Waghorn to cut his vacation short, paying even money. The office of the President of the United States regretted that he was too busy to pay personal attention to the situation. They had referred the letter to the Prime Minister of Canada. The office of the Prime Minister wrote that they had referred both Sidney's letter and the President's letter to the OPP.

Sidney opened the last letter, the one from the OPP.

Dear Mr. Weston,

Perhaps you have not understood our message. We do not wish to receive letters from you, either directly or through any head of state. We hate receiving letters from you. We destroy them.
Sincerely,
Ontario Provincial Police

"I can't understand the OPP," mused Sidney incredulously. "They just don't seem to appreciate the seriousness of the situation."

"What? What about the OPP? What's going on?"

"Nothing."

Sidney's orderly mind made a mental list of what he had to do. He had to mail his latest batch of letters, and find another phone to warn the air base about the inside man. Soon the laxatives would wear off and Parson and Bishop would be back in action. Sometime this afternoon he had to start planting those homing pins.

Tom stared intently at his brother. Sidney had the afternoon off, but so did he. And he planned to stick to Sidney like glue.

* * *

Captain Snider had arranged for Lieutenant Simcha to sit at Table 19 with Waghorn and Vishnik. There he sat, thoroughly enjoying his lunch, although he had absolutely no idea what that

woman, Miss Fuller, was talking about. Something to do with spies? He decided not to pay any attention to it, as it would only serve to confuse him. After all, he was on a very important mission here. And since he didn't really understand the mission, it would be wise to keep his head clear.

Bert Cobber looked up from his soup and spoke to Simcha. "Hey there, mate, could you please pass the bread?"

"Certainly, *sir!*" He handed the basket to Cobber.

"Thanks."

"You're welcome, *sir!*" This cover was going to be easy, thought Simcha. He fit right in.

Richard Knight, one eyebrow raised, was gazing at Simcha in speculation. It had taken him but a few seconds to spot the young man's military manner. Apparently Sidney Weston had stirred up the air base to the point where Snider had sent in an agent. Knight made a mental note to investigate further.

Miss Fuller surveyed the table with a synthetic smile. "How do you think our little spy game is going, Mr. Kitzel?"

For the first time since his arrival at the hotel Mr. Kitzel was having a very light meal. "I'm sick and tired of talking about spies all the time. Let's talk about something interesting—like my daughter Sarah." He reached into his pocket. "Here's her picture. Cute, eh?"

The picture was passed around and admired.

"This is a photograph of Shirley Temple," Knight pointed out.

"Well—uh—you noticed the resemblance, eh?" Kitzel stammered. "I told you she was cute. Of course, she's a lot older now. Started college last year." He looked at Miss Fuller. "It cost me a fortune, but I got a big deduction off my *income tax*."

"Vishnik likes spy game better," piped up the artist. "Both are stupid, but this is boring."

Lawrence Waghorn leaped into the conversation. "I think income tax is very interesting," he announced. If this discussion replaced the spy game, on which he was basing his script, it would serve Miss Fuller right.

"Yeah," agreed Bert Cobber. Any talk of spies made him edgy.

"You see?" announced Mr. Kitzel triumphantly. "Let's tell income tax stories."

"Right," agreed Waghorn jubilantly. "Last year I got thirty dollars back on my return."

"How nice for you," commented Knight dryly. He was having difficulty keeping his amusement under control.

Miss Fuller looked sly. "I wonder if spies pay income tax."

Simcha looked around in confusion. These were very strange people. Could that be what Snider had been talking about?

"To heck with income tax," snorted Cobber. "The thing to do is hire yourself a smart accountant and cheat!"

"Never!" thundered Mr. Kitzel. "It's a privilege to pay income tax!"

"Vishnik agrees with him," said the artist, indicating Cobber. "Phooey on income tax. Phooey on spies. Phooey on the creep who stole Vishnik's dog! Phooey on this stupid hotel!"

"I've paid exactly the right amount of income tax since I got my first job," boasted Mr. Kitzel. "And that was a long time ago. It's a shame Sarah's expenses were so high last year, so I couldn't pay that much tax. But this year will be much better, because she found a summer job."

"On the Good Ship Lollipop, no doubt," said Knight.

"Exactly where is Sarah right now?" asked Waghorn with feigned interest.

"Sarah? Oh, I left her at home but Mrs. Goldberg comes over once a day to feed her and let her out if the weather's nice." Mr. Kitzel realized his mistake and clamped both hands over his mouth.

It all dawned on Knight with amazing clarity. Kitzel had claimed a pet as a daughter on his tax return. Now he was afraid Fuller was an investigating tax agent. A less sophisticated man would have laughed out loud. Knight merely smiled.

Cobber laughed out loud. "What kind of a daughter have you got?"

Kitzel was bright red and stuttering. "College girl. Very studious," he managed.

"She isn't a spy, is she?" asked Miss Fuller.

"Oh, shut up!" mumbled Waghorn under his breath.

"The man is crazy, yes?" asked Vishnik.

"Possibly, *sir!*" said Simcha smartly. Were they talking about income tax, or were they back to spies again?

Knight looked at Simcha sympathetically. The boy was obviously out of his depth.

* * *

Lawrence Waghorn relaxed in a lounge chair by the pool, trying to get in some sun before he started on the afternoon's writing.

Sidney Weston walked along the edge of the pool. In front of Waghorn he dropped to one knee to tighten his loose shoelace. Waghorn did not see a hand steal under the lounge chair and jam a homing pin into the rubber sole of his running shoe.

Tom emerged from behind a bush. Sidney had done something to Waghorn's shoe. He had to find out what it was and, if possible, undo it. He strolled nonchalantly up to the patio, then dropped to his belly and began to slither along the row of chairs. Once under Waghorn's chair, he grasped the shoe and examined it. There was a tiny white-headed pin jammed into the sole. He pulled at it with his fingernails—it would not budge. He dug at it with both thumbnails, but it

133

was firmly embedded in the rubber. He tried pushing the rubber down, but the pin went down with it. Desperately he put the shoe to his mouth, clamped his front teeth around the head of the pin and pulled. The pin slid smoothly out, but the shoe sailed out of Tom's hands through the air and plopped into the deep end of the pool. It sank like a rock.

Waghorn jumped up. "My shoe! Who did that?"

Tom emerged sheepishly from under the chair, the pin still in his mouth.

"Uh—I did, sir. It was an accident." The pin fell out of his mouth and rolled into a crack in the pavement.

"You! Aren't you the kid who spilled orange juice all over me yesterday? What are you trying to do?"

"I'm terribly sorry, sir."

"What's going on? Has *she* hired you to try and psych me out? Well, you march right back there and tell Fuller that it won't work! Come on, now, beat it!"

In the pool Lieutenant Simcha surfaced, holding the shoe. He pulled himself over the side and walked, dripping, over to Tom. "I believe you dropped this, *sir!*"

Waghorn grabbed the shoe. "It's mine. Thanks."

"You're welcome, *sir!*"

Tom slunk off, mortified that it was he and not Sidney who was creating a disturbance.

134

*   *   *

Cobber was sitting leafing through a girlie magazine when there was a knock at his door.

"Who is it?"

"Knight."

Frantically the pilot snatched up the photographs of the Osiris flight manual and hid his magazine among them.

"Come on in, mate," he called genially.

Knight entered the room.

"I've been studying real hard, Dick," Cobber announced proudly from the depths of the plans and, of course, his magazine.

"I can see that," said Knight sardonically. He reached over and snatched the magazine out of the sheaf of pictures. "Which one? The blonde or the brunette?"

"Aw, mate!"

"Save it, Cobber. You will know these plans by tomorrow, because tomorrow I shall burn them."

"Gee, Dick, I don't know if you're giving me enough—"

"You've had time to spare. Tomorrow we will begin to discuss the actual operation. You will learn to keep pace. Things rarely go well for people who jeopardize my work."

"I'll learn the stuff, Dick. Hey, what was all that crazy talk about at lunch?"

Knight smiled. "It is a very long and involved story, Cobber. You wouldn't understand it. Suf-

fice it to say that it is nothing you need concern yourself with."

"But what about that Simcha guy?" Cobber persisted. "He looks a lot like a soldier to me."

Knight had just finished searching Simcha's room, and the man had indeed been sent from Trillium Base in response to the Weston boy's warning. He could pose absolutely no threat, however, since he seemed not only not to understand his assignment, but also to be ignoring it. When last seen, he had been taking disco lessons; before that, he had spent hours at the pool. The man was too stupid to be a danger. He was also a failure as an agent. Even Cobber had seen through his cover.

"Forget about Simcha," Knight said finally. "He is the second biggest idiot I have ever encountered. And Cobber, one last thing. Do not disturb me today. I am going to be extremely busy."

"Sure, mate. I'll just stay here and study."

The door closed and Cobber's eyes lit up craftily. No way was he going to sit here and be bored all day. He was going to have a little excursion into town. After all, Dick was going to be busy. And what Dick didn't know wouldn't hurt him.

*   *   *

Sidney walked across the front lawn to where Vishnik sat painting.

"Vishnik did not order drink," snapped the artist without missing a brush stroke.

"Compliments of the hotel."

"In that case, Vishnik accepts." He picked up the glass from the bar tray.

From behind a clump of bushes peered Tom. Oh, no! Sidney was delivering drinks again! He jumped out of the bushes and dashed across the lawn. Reaching Vishnik in a wild bound, he grabbed the glass from the astounded artist's lips and spilled the contents out on the grass.

In one swift motion Sidney inserted the homing pin into the collar of Vishnik's painting smock.

"What kind of stupid hotel is this?" raved Vishnik. "They give with one hand and take away with other!"

"You didn't want to drink that, did you?" stammered Tom.

"Go away. Vishnik cannot paint."

"You were trying to feed poor Mr. Vishnik some of that laxative!" Tom accused as he and Sidney walked away.

"No," said his brother in amazement. "Mr. Parson asked me to deliver a complimentary drink, that's all."

"Do you expect me to believe that, Sidney? You're off duty."

"I volunteered to do it anyway. It's no big deal."

With a sinking heart, Tom looked at the front entrance of the hotel. There stood Parson, burn-

ing with indignation. Tom ran up to his boss. Sidney walked off in another direction.

"Weston, what on earth were you trying to prove out there? Why would you do such a thing?"

"I'm sorry, sir," said Tom. "I'll get Mr. Vishnik another drink."

"At once, if you please. The poor man is terribly upset about his dog. Get out there and cheer him up. Talk to him. Make him enjoy his stay here at Pine Grove."

Tom ran off, got the drink and raced back across the lawn towards Vishnik.

As the artist arched and craned to examine his work, he felt something scratching against his neck. He reached back and pulled out the pin. "What is this? I should kill those creeps in laundry! Vishnik could have been stabbed! Then world would be deprived of great art!" He tossed the pin contemptuously onto the ground.

Tom jogged up. "Here's your drink, Mr. Vishnik."

Vishnik took the glass and looked around warily. "Where is other one who looks exactly like you to take away?"

Tom grinned sheepishly. "No, this one you can keep."

Vishnik took a sip and returned to his work.

"That's a very beautiful painting you're working on, sir." Tom craned his neck to get a better view. It looked like two people taking a bubble bath in an egg.

138

"Bah! Vishnik cannot paint without companionship of Vishnik's dog!"

Tom swallowed. "Well, anyway, have a nice day." He began to walk away. "*Ow!*" He lifted up his right foot. Embedded in the sole was a pin exactly like the one he had removed from Waghorn's shoe. Angrily he jammed the pin deep into the ground and stomped off.

* * *

Wings Weinberg and Captain Snider stepped out of the movie theatre and walked towards their car in the parking lot.

"Pretty good movie, eh, Wings?"

"Yeah," agreed Wings enthusiastically. "I loved the part where Bill tracked down the man who'd been haunting him for years. What a great murder scene!"

Snider got into the car, Colonel Cartwright's staff car, and unlocked Wings' door.

Wings' gaze suddenly locked on a blue Plymouth sedan at the edge of the sidewalk. His eyes bulged, his mouth dropped again.

"It's—Bert Cobber!"

"Where?" cried Snider.

Wings pointed wordlessly at the Plymouth, which was pulling away.

"Come on, Wings! Get in the car!"

With a screech of tires, the big Oldsmobile whipped out of the parking lot and onto the street behind Cobber.

At the wheel of Knight's rented car, Cobber checked the rearview mirror. Wow, it was Wings —Wings and that captain guy! Oh, no! They were chasing him! If he got caught, Dick would kill him! He wasn't even supposed to be in town! He speeded up and began to weave in and out of the traffic, widening the gap between the two cars. Snider, too, began to accelerate.

With a squeal of his tires, Cobber turned onto the highway against the light, narrowly missing a red car, which spun around in traffic to avoid him. Snider whipped around the corner as well, leaning on the horn to warn people out of the way. He sideswiped the red car, leaving a long scratch along the length of the Colonel's. Once on the highway, he floored the pedal with determination.

"We're going to catch that guy if it kills us!"

Wings held on, gazing fixedly at the car up ahead and at what he knew to be the back of Cobber's head.

Cobber noticed the Oldsmobile still on his tail. "This'll shake 'em!" He wrenched the wheel around and the car flew over the median. Making a complete turn, he roared down the highway in the opposite direction, passing Wings and Snider and averting his face to avoid recognition.

Snider spun his own steering wheel and, with a squeal, was over the median, leaving the muffler clanking behind. The sand and gravel flew as Snider's car hit the soft shoulder. A rock flew up and cracked Wings' side window.

140

Cobber checked his mirror. The Olds was still there. He leaned on the horn, but two trucks blocking his way ahead would not permit him to pass. Snider and Wings were getting larger and larger in the mirror. Suddenly Cobber signalled to the left and veered sharply right, tearing off the road through a cedar-rail fence and jouncing across a well-cultivated cornfield, spraying mud in all directions.

Snider gritted his teeth and followed, flicking on his windshield wipers to clear away the dirt Cobber was kicking up. The wipers snapped off and were gone. Snider was driving completely blind. Hastily he rolled down his window and stuck his head out. There was a barn coming! With a crash, the car smashed through the barn door, wood splinters and hay flying everywhere. The cows looked on without interest as the Oldsmobile shot straight through the barn and out the other side.

Snider brought the car to a halt to get his bearings.

"There he is!" Wings pointed to Cobber's blue Plymouth working its way back through the field towards the highway.

Snider floored the accelerator, spinning the back wheels, sending mud and hay spraying everywhere. The car took off, shattering the corner of a chicken coop, and hit the highway, once more on Cobber's tail. Both cars whipped past the *Pinedale City Limits* sign back into town.

Hearing sirens, Snider checked his rearview

mirror. Two motorcycle policemen were on his tail.

Cobber was pressing his gas pedal all the way to the floor. "Won't this thing go any faster?" Ahead of him he saw the orange jacket of a crossing guard who, holding a *Stop* sign, was strolling into the middle of the street followed by a line of small children with sun hats and lunch pails. "Oh, no! Kids!" Desperately Cobber jerked the wheel to the right, flying across the front lawn of a school and bumping back onto the road past the crosswalk where the day-campers were crossing.

Snider followed, bouncing across the lawn and flattening the Elmer-the-Safety-Elephant flagpole. The collision left a huge rent in the grille and snapped off the hood ornament, which flew back and cracked the windshield.

The Olds bumped back onto the road in pursuit of Cobber, followed now by three motorcycle police and two patrol cars, all with sirens wailing.

Cobber looked ahead. A turning bus blocked the intersection. Once again he spun the wheel, ending up in a narrow alley. He barely had a chance to see the sign: *Dead End.*

"Abandon car!" he bellowed as he jumped out into a nearby garbage bin. The car continued on at top speed to smash into a brick wall at the end of the alley.

Cobber leaped out of the garbage bin, clambered over the wall and was gone before the military staff car whipped around the corner of the

alley, bouncing from wall to wall with a screech of metal. It smashed off the bottom of a fire escape and came to rest in a huge pile of garbage.

Six large policemen approached the car, guns drawn.

"All right, you two! You're under arrest!"

*   *   *

Richard Knight had spent the day sleeping. He had ordered dinner from room service and was sitting watching the local six o'clock news on television.

Our top story today, announced the newscaster, *is a wild car chase through Pinedale. Police are still looking for the driver of this car.* The screen showed a picture of the complete wreckage of a blue car in an alley. Knight's keen eyes picked out the licence plate. That was his car! *The exact details of the chase are not known. However, police think the chase began at around three o'clock this afternoon . . .*

Knight pushed his dinner tray aside, switched off the TV set and knocked on Cobber's door.

Cobber opened it, all smiles. "Hi, there, mate. I was just going down for dinner."

Knight entered the room, slammed the door, grabbed Cobber by the collar and threw him into an armchair.

"Cobber, where is the car?"

"Funny you should ask, mate. I've been mean-

ing to tell you about that. I had a little accident."

"I saw," said Knight icily. "You were the top story on the news. You totalled the car in an alley—my rented car."

"They can't trace it to you, can they, Dick?"

"Of course not," said Knight. "I rented it with falsified identification. But that is hardly the point. What were you doing in Pinedale when I specifically ordered you to stay here?"

"Well, you know, I got kind of bored and . . ." His voice trailed off at the expression on Knight's face.

"Pray continue."

Cobber had an idea. "Well, you know, Dick, we pilots—we're kind of high-strung. You just can't keep us cooped up like this. Heck, they took Wings to town."

Knight stiffened. "That was Weinberg who was chasing you? You idiot! He can identify you!"

"Oh, he never got a good look at me," said Cobber airily.

"Really? Then why did he chase you?"

Cobber shrugged. "Beats me. I walked back so no one could track me," he added proudly. "Anyway, I'm really sorry about the car, Dick."

"Cobber, perhaps you do not appreciate the seriousness of the situation. You see, this means you have twice disobeyed my orders. Only two other people have ever done that—and they are both regrettably no longer with us. Do you understand what I am saying?"

"Yeah, mate."

"Good. You see, while I do need you right now, there *are* other pilots. If you persist in jeopardizing the operation, I shall exercise my option to select one."

"Yeah, mate. I get you."

"Now you will study." From his inside jacket pocket Knight produced a small hand gun and pointed it at Cobber's head. "And I shall sit here and make sure that you do."

As Cobber began to go over the photographs, Knight wondered if perhaps he had made a mistake in not disposing of the man. Well, it was too late now.

* * *

"All right, Hayes, it's ten o'clock. Where are they?"

"I'm sure they're just having a good time in town, sir," soothed the corporal.

"In a place like Pinedale?" barked Cartwright. "Impossible! Something's happened to Weinberg. I know it!"

Both heard it at the same time—the roar of a loud motor.

"A tank," said Cartwright. "Who's driving a tank on my base?"

Hayes was first to the window. "Colonel!"

Cartwright headed for the door. "I'm going to tell those fools to get their tank off my base."

"But, sir—"

Cartwright ran out the door. "Now listen, you —" His mouth dropped open. A wreck was ap-

proaching, roaring, bucking and backfiring. Steam spewed from the radiator; the entire body was scratched, dented and caked with mud and hay, and most of the windows were gone; one loose headlight flickered feebly, and the tires wobbled dangerously.

Cartwright stared. Pushing the car was Snider and a few of the sentries. At the wheel, his eyes glazed over, his face chalk-white, sat Wings Weinberg.

By the time Cartwright could make out the Oldsmobile logo through the mud, he didn't want to any more.

"*SNIDER!*"

Snider limped forward and saluted feebly. "Sorry we're late, sir. We ran into some trouble."

Cartwright's face was purple. "Snider, is that my staff car?"

"I'm afraid so, sir. Come on, Wings," Snider called. "Let's go into the Colonel's office and explain everything."

The three men entered the office and Cartwright seated himself at his desk. "This had better be good!" he snapped, shaking with rage.

"Well, sir, we were coming out of the movie," explained Snider, "when Wings saw Bert Cobber. One way or the other, I wanted to find out who the guy was, so we got into the car and went after him. But he saw us and took off. He did some crazy things and, sir, in the heat of the chase I guess I got carried away."

"In my staff car! You smashed up my car

chasing a ghost? Snider, it may interest you that I had Headquarters do a computer check on that guy Bert Cobber. He has not been seen or heard from since his graduation, and is presumed to be dead. You hear that? Dead! You took off after some innocent guy and he panicked and ran away!"

"That was Bert Cobber," said Wings positively. "I recognized him. And besides, nobody else could possibly drive like that."

"Certainly not Snider," said Cartwright bitterly. "But if this happened this afternoon, where have you been until now?"

"Well, we were both out of uniform," offered Snider, "and the police didn't believe—"

"The police! You were arrested?"

"It took a few hours before one of the guards recognized Wings," Snider admitted.

"Recognized him!" The commanding officer was horrified. "Do you mean this is going to be in the papers?"

"No, sir," said Snider. "We convinced them that Wings' mission here is top secret."

Cartwright sank back into his chair, grateful for something. "Well, at least you had that much sense. All right, Weinberg, you may as well go off to bed. You haven't been getting enough rest lately. And remember—Cobber is dead."

Wings left, disbelief showing plainly on his face.

"Snider," shouted the C.O. when the pilot was gone, "what are you trying to do? I sent you to

town to show the guy a good time and keep him relaxed. I didn't say to involve him in a high-speed chase—and I certainly didn't give you permission to wreck my car!"

Snider swallowed hard. "Colonel, if Bert Cobber is dead, why did that guy run from us?"

"I don't know. Maybe he'd just robbed a bank or something and thought you were the police. Who cares? The thing is, you went out and got Weinberg wound up even worse than before. And wrecked my car in the process! Snider, if he flubs that test I'll bust you right down to private!"

"Yes, sir."

There was a timid knock on the door. "Captain Snider," said Hayes, "if you're finished—"

"Oh, he's finished, all right!" muttered Cartwright.

"The guy called again, Captain," the corporal announced. "He must have found another phone."

"What did he say?"

"Did he say anything about wrecked cars?" growled Cartwright.

"He mentioned the usual about Parson, Bishop, Vishnik and Waghorn, and he told us to be extra careful because the spy ring has an 'inside man' on the base."

Snider stiffened. "An inside man? Who?"

"Probably you, Snider," the Colonel put in. "Who else would take a base vehicle and mash it into hamburger?"

Hayes shrugged. "He didn't give a name. But

148

then something funny happened, sir. I can't understand it. It sounded like a struggle for the phone, and a lady came on and said, 'Don't forget to watch out for Mr. Kitzel.' Then the line went dead."

"Not another one!" Snider groaned. "Who's Mr. Kitzel?"

"I checked the lists and he's a guest at the hotel too." Hayes looked up. "Sir, things are getting really weird, aren't they?"

"Things got weird when they gave Snider a driver's licence," seethed the Colonel.

"Pretty weird," Snider agreed. "Have you heard from Simcha?"

"No, sir. I tried to call him, but he wasn't in his room."

"He's probably busy tailing all those people," Snider decided. "We'll get him tomorrow."

In fact, Lieutenant Simcha was at that moment dining and dancing in the Pine Grove Flamenco Lounge.

* * *

Tom Weston let himself into the twins' room after the day's work. He threw off his jacket and began to prepare for bed, ignoring the growling coming from the two dogs.

Sidney was seated at the desk, deep in thought, killing time until it was safe to take Z-2 and Z-4 for their walk. "You know, Tom," he said finally, "you've been getting into a lot of trouble lately.

You'd better watch yourself or we could lose our jobs."

Tom's first reaction was to go for Sidney's throat. Instead, he took the edge of his blanket, bit down hard and counted to ten. After all, Sidney was right. Tom *had* been getting into a lot of trouble lately. But he had only been doing it to keep Sidney *out* of trouble. Life was so unfair.

9

Fun! Fun! Fun!

Richard Knight sat patiently outside the manager's office. Parson was already occupied with a caller and the two voices, one shouting, one soothing, could be heard through the closed door.

"It is now three days since Vishnik's dog has been separated from Vishnik! What is stupid hotel doing about finding Vishnik's dog?"

"Please, Mr. Vishnik, we're doing all we can. I haven't found my Blackie, you know, so I understand your feelings. Hotel security is doing everything possible, and they've notified the local police and the OPP to be on the lookout for two retrievers."

"Why doesn't stupid hotel security look in all rooms for Vishnik's dog?" demanded the angry artist.

Parson looked righteous. "Now, now, sir, we can't violate people's privacy. Besides, I'm sure no one at the hotel would steal our dogs."

"Vishnik will not be bought off with free

drinks! Vishnik will give stupid hotel forty-eight hours to find Vishnik's dog, or Vishnik will look for Vishnik's dog himself!" And with that he stormed out of the office, muttering under his breath.

Knight knocked politely on the half-open door.

"Come in."

He entered and sat down opposite Parson's desk.

The manager looked at him nervously. "Well, Mr. Knight, what seems to be the trouble? You—uh—don't have a dog, do you?"

"No." Knight smiled broadly. "I have no problems. I would just like to tell you what a wonderful time I'm having at your hotel. I've had holidays at many resorts, but this is by far the best."

Parson leaned back in the chair in sheer relief. "I'm very happy to hear that, sir."

"Oh, yes," Knight exclaimed enthusiastically, "your facilities are marvellous, your food superb, your staff excellent and your entertainment fabulous. Why, that midnight wiener roast you have planned is sheer genius."

Parson regarded him blankly. "Midnight wiener roast?"

"Yes, it's great! Everyone is excited about it and I know the children can't wait for tomorrow night."

"Tomorrow night?"

"I've never seen a more inventive, better planned event. It shows excellent management. That's why I thought I'd come down here and congratulate you. Since people are so quick to

point out the negative aspects, when I saw something as positive as your wiener roast, I felt I just had to mention it."

Parson smiled weakly. "Well, thank you very much, Mr. Knight."

Knight got up. "You're most entirely welcome, Mr. Parson. See you at the wiener roast."

Parson sat for a moment, staring blankly at the now-empty chair opposite his desk. Midnight wiener roast? What midnight wiener roast?

He got up and walked out to the reception desk. "Delores, what's this about a midnight wiener roast?"

The woman stared at him. "Sir?"

"A wiener roast. Are we having one?"

"Not that I know of," said the clerk. She turned to the hotel cashier. "Margaret, did you hear anything about a wiener roast?"

"A wiener roast? No. Why?"

"Mr. Parson says we might be having one."

"I've never heard anything about it."

The clerk turned back to Parson. "No," she confirmed, "we've never heard about any wiener roast, sir."

The chief cook came storming down the hall, across the lobby and up to the desk, white apron flapping and cap awry.

"Mr. Parson, what's all this?"

"Something wrong, Edward?" asked Parson coldly. The kitchen staff was not supposed to appear in the lobby while on duty.

"Something is very wrong, sir," said Edward angrily. "Do you know what was just delivered to

153

my kitchen? One thousand wieners, that's what! And a thousand buns!"

"Wieners?" chorused Parson and the desk clerk.

"Yes, wieners! Not to mention four 500-packs of marshmallows and thirty-five cases of potato chips! And get this—fifty litres of pink lemonade and fifty of grape juice! I mean, sir, with all due respect, I'm not running a fast-food joint! What am I going to do with all that junk food?"

Parson looked bewildered. "Who signed the purchase order?"

Edward stared at him. "You did!" He produced the piece of paper. There, at the bottom of a Pine Grove requisition, was Walter Parson's signature.

Across the lobby Tom Weston arrived, armed with a hammer and nails. He began to put up a large bright-orange poster.

Parson squinted and read:

COME TO THE BIG EVENT!
MIDNIGHT BONFIRE AND WIENER ROAST
Bring the kids!
Bring the whole family!
FUN! FUN! FUN!
Eat, drink, dance to the music of
THE UPTOWN SCHOOLHOUSE JAZZ BAND
Mammoth fireworks display!
Games! Prizes! Singsongs!
FREE BEER!
Wednesday Night   11:00 PM
1st Tee   Pine Grove Golf Course
DON'T MISS IT!

Parson looked at the cook sternly. "Don't you keep up with what's going on around here? It's for the wiener roast, of course. See?" He pointed at the poster. "And because I was ill, we've all let this go too long without proper planning. I want to see the whole staff hard at work. The guests are really looking forward to this, and it has to be perfect!"

He returned to his office and began leafing through his memos. What was this? A permit from the local fire department to hold a fireworks display. Attached to it was a note saying that two experienced firemen would be on hand to supervise things. And what was this? The contract signing the Uptown Schoolhouse Jazz Band! They were a nine-piece band, so the contract said. There was a copy of the food order—and an order to Brewers' Retail for four hundred bottles of beer! Also, an order to Petroff Lumber Company for four cords of wood, and fifteen hundred roasting sticks! And here was a bill for five hundred party hats, five hundred noisemakers and a thousand balloons, accompanied by five tanks of compressed helium!

Yes, there was definitely a wiener roast. Each one of these documents sported his own signature, plain as day. There was no doubt that he had planned all this. How could he have forgotten? He must have been sicker than he thought.

All right, he said inwardly. Pull yourself together. You have a big event to plan.

* * *

Richard Knight and Bert Cobber sat over Cobber's metal wastebasket, which contained the flaming photographs of the flight manual for the Osiris HE2.

"Well, that's that," said Knight. "It certainly took you long enough. Now we come to the actual operation. You'll have to learn this very quickly, Cobber. The Osiris test is scheduled for Thursday afternoon. We are going into action Wednesday night."

"But, Dick," protested Cobber. "Isn't Wednesday the night we're having the big wiener roast?"

"Precisely."

"Mate, how can we steal the Osiris with the whole hotel sitting on the golf course? That wiener roast was a bit of bad luck."

"Oh?" said Knight, one eyebrow raised. "Who do you think planned it?"

Cobber shrugged. "The hotel, I guess. Maybe that guy Parson or—" He stopped in mid-sentence. "*You?*"

"Naturally. I personally ordered the food and the balloons, hats and noisemakers, hired the band and ordered posters and handbills printed."

"But how did you do that?" asked Cobber, amazed.

"I sign a very creditable 'Walter Parson,'" said Knight with satisfaction. "I think the man might be hard-put to discover the fraud himself. Oh, yes, and I also arranged a permit for the fireworks, of which I ordered a considerable amount."

"But why, Dick?"

156

"For a diversion. The entire hotel will be partying madly on a piece of property adjacent to the air base. All the guests will be involved in the festivities, and if this party is as loud and wild as I expect, the sentries will be more interested in what's going on than in guarding the Osiris. I shall have no trouble getting you to the plane. And if you have any competence whatsoever as a pilot, you will have no trouble flying to where I tell you—where you'll be paid and spirited out of the country."

"I can fly it, mate, don't worry," promised Cobber. "Where to?"

Knight spread a large map out between them.

"All right, Cobber, now here is Trillium Base ..."

*　*　*

Sidney slipped a handbill advertising the wiener roast under the last door in the corridor, darted down to the kitchen and nabbed two portions of prime rib roast. This time there was no danger of being caught. The kitchen staff was far too concerned with wieners to care about anything else. When he reached his room, he found Tom sitting outside waiting for him. The two entered together and Sidney tossed the dogs their dinner.

"Only five letters today," Tom commented. "You must be slipping."

Sidney opened the letters eagerly. There was another from Bruce of the RCMP. He acknowledged all the latest details in a friendly manner,

but still refused to assign any men to the case. *What do you need men for when you've got that devastating laxative of yours?* he explained.

Connie, from NATO, seemed a little confused, since she suggested that Parson and Vishnik be taken to the veterinarian, and that Z-2 and Z-4 be reported to the local authorities. In any case, she had sent a photocopy of Sidney's letter to the OPP.

Steve, from Norad, was rather upset that he had lost his bet about Z-5, and bitterly pointed out that a certain private in the mail room had successfully predicted the laxative incident and made a killing in the pool. Steve didn't mind losing, but confidentially asked Sidney to keep such large sums of money away from the enlisted men, especially when he, a general, was coming away empty-handed. In any case, Steve had transferred his stakes to Vishnik's nervous breakdown, a reasonably safe bet at two to one. He expected to recoup his losses and make a profit befitting his rank.

Mark wrote that the Department of National Defence was quite content to leave the handling of this case in the capable hands of Sidney Weston. After all, he had certainly handled Parson and Bishop with great expertise. There was no reason to move in and take over the case from someone who was doing so well with it single-handedly.

Sidney opened the last letter. It was from the OPP.

Dear Mr. Weston,

We are finding it very hard to believe that you still persist in writing us letters. We do not want any more letters. We dislike them and we dislike you. Leave us alone.

The Ontario Provincial Police

Carefully he pocketed the letters and sat down on his bed. He stared curiously at a copy of the handbill advertising the wiener roast.

"Tom, what do you think about this wiener roast?"

"What do I think? What's to think? It sounds like a good party and a whole lot of extra work."

Sidney frowned. "There's something fishy about the whole thing. Somehow, a wiener roast is not Pine Grove's style."

"Maybe that's why they're doing it," suggested Tom, "to cut away from the fancy stuff for once. Everyone enjoys a fling now and then—everyone but you, that is. You're too busy suspecting people of plots against the western world!"

Sidney lay back, deep in thought. He didn't trust this wiener roast. There was something distinctly wrong, but he couldn't put his finger on it. He racked his brain but could not figure out the connection between the wiener roast and Waghorn's plans.

His disciplined mind shifted off the subject. He shouldn't confuse himself by thinking about the wiener roast until there was evidence that a

connection existed. There was already enough to think about. He had to get the rest of the homing pins planted before assigned duty on the party took all his time.

Sidney glanced at his brother. Tom seemed to have dozed off. He reached into his jacket pocket and palmed two homing pins, then glanced back at Tom. He was definitely asleep. Sidney put the dogs in the bathroom and tiptoed out the door.

Cautiously Tom opened his right eye and scouted the room. His brother was gone. He groaned inwardly. Sidney was on the loose again, and it was up to him to follow and make sure he didn't do anything stupid. Like those pins. Tom frowned in exasperation. What *were* those pins?

He left the room, falling to his knees behind the garbage can until Sidney disappeared down the stairs. Then, keeping a discreet distance, he followed.

*   *   *

There were quite a few people in the Pine Grove gymnasium that morning and Dave Bishop, clad as always in his red Olympic track suit, was strolling around checking on the guests at their various activities.

From around the door frame Sidney took in the scene for a moment, then jogged purposefully across the polished floor, brushing past Bishop and depositing a small homing pin near the zipper of his track-suit jacket.

160

Tom, crouched in another doorway, watched his brother leave the gym. Strolling into the room, he slipped into the group around Bishop and quickly spied the tiny white pin. How was he going to get it?

"Excuse me, Dave," said one girl. "Would you show us how to climb the ropes?"

"Sure." Bishop removed his jacket and gave it to Tom, who had the presence of mind to stretch a hand out.

No problem, thought Tom as Bishop flexed his muscles in preparation. He found the pin and pulled at it. The tip was stuck in the zipper.

"The secret is to grip with your ankles," said Bishop as Tom continued to struggle with the pin.

Abruptly the pin came loose. Tom's hand slipped and struck the back of the athletic director's track pants.

"Owww!" Bishop shot up the rope like a monkey.

There was applause from the small group of watchers.

"Oh, I can do that, *sir*," said Lieutenant Simcha. Grasping a second rope, he imitated Bishop's cry of agony and scrambled to the top.

Tom slunk away, kicking the pin underneath the vaulting horse. He had better hurry. Sidney had a head start.

* * *

"This stupid hotel is driving Vishnik crazy!" exclaimed the artist over lunch. "Vishnik's dog is still missing, but are they looking for Vishnik's dog? No. They are planning stupid midnight wiener roast!"

"Now, now," said Richard Knight. "We're all very sorry that your dog is missing, but activities can't stop because of it. I for one am looking forward to the midnight wiener roast."

"Me too," said Bert Cobber.

"It should be very enjoyable, *sir!*" added Simcha.

Mr. Kitzel pushed away his soup and placed a briefcase on the table. "I've brought along a summary of my tax history," he announced. "I called my accountant for all my returns since 1946."

"Eat them!" barked Vishnik.

Miss Fuller looked at Mr. Kitzel. "Who wants to see your silly old tax returns?"

"Don't you?"

"No!" she exclaimed. "I want to play the spy game. We haven't played that in a while."

"Let's keep it that way," suggested Lawrence Waghorn. "Mr. Kitzel, *I'd* like to see one of those returns. Let's say—1957."

Kitzel glared at him. "Mind your own business." He looked strangely at Miss Fuller, then put his briefcase back under his chair and returned to his soup. She was making it tough for him, eh? How could he prove to her that he was an honest taxpayer—especially when he wasn't?

Parson walked up to the table, a friendly smile

on his face. "And how is everything here at Table 19?"

"Terrible!" growled Vishnik.

"Very good, *sir!*" replied Simcha.

"Excellent, excellent," said Richard Knight genially. "We were just talking about how much fun the wiener roast is going to be."

Parson fairly beamed. "Oh, I'm delighted to hear that so many guests are looking forward to it. Other people have also been displaying enthusiasm. If everything goes well, we're considering making it an annual event here at Pine Grove."

Cobber laughed out loud and received a kick under the table for his indiscretion.

"Yes," said Miss Fuller, "there's nothing like sitting around a big bonfire swapping spy stories."

Waghorn snorted in disgust.

"You mean income tax stories," put in Mr. Kitzel.

"No," said Miss Fuller firmly. "Spy stories."

"Income tax stories!"

"Spy stories!"

"Income tax!"

"Spy!"

"Now, now," said Parson soothingly, "I'm sure there will be time for both spy and—uh—income tax stories." He drifted off towards Table 20.

* * *

"It's beautiful," said Wings Weinberg, gazing up at the hyperellipsoid nose cone of the Osiris HE2. He, Colonel Cartwright and Captain Snider were

163

in Hangar B checking on the engineers' progress.

"It sure is," agreed Cartwright. He turned to the chief engineer. "Is everything on schedule?"

"Right on schedule, Colonel. On the tick. This baby'll be revved up and ready to fly first thing Thursday afternoon. Right, Wings?"

Wings grinned. "You've never let me down," he confirmed.

"Good," said Cartwright, doubly happy that being with the Osiris and his technical crew did wonders for Wings' attitude. "General McAllister and the Norad people arrive sometime Wednesday. We want to impress them with our efficiency here at Trillium."

The outdoor P.A. system rang with Hayes' voice: "Captain Snider, please report to the commander's office. Urgent. Captain Snider."

"I'll grab the jeep," said Snider, heading for the door.

"You'll walk!" growled Cartwright.

"But, sir—he said it's urgent!"

"Then run, but no jeep, Snider. You've destroyed your last base vehicle."

Red-faced, Snider ran out of Hangar B, out of the hangar area, around the living quarters and into Cartwright's office.

"What's the trouble, Hayes? Did Simcha call?"

"No, sir. Still nothing from Simcha, and I can't reach him. But I'm trying every half hour. *He* called again." Hayes switched on the tape. "Sir, you'd better hear this."

The now-familiar voice whispered, "It's me.

164

Have you captured the inside man yet?"

"No," came Hayes' voice.

"Well, do you know who he is yet?"

"No," said Hayes.

"I'll describe him for you. He's about a hundred and seventy-six to a hundred and seventy-six and a half centimetres tall and quite heavily built—I'd estimate approximately eighty-three and a quarter kilograms. He's fairly young—about thirty-one years old. He's a captain, and the insignia on his sleeve was 'Security.' His eyes are green, his hair is medium-brown, and he has all his own teeth. He has no major identifying marks save a small cut on his left hand—and there was a spot of mustard on his tie when I saw him."

"But that's *me!*" cried Snider.

"Do you know who this might be?" asked the voice on the tape.

"Ah—er—I'll have to check personnel files," stammered Hayes' voice.

"I'm sorry I couldn't get a better description, but I only saw him for a few seconds. Hey, there's Parson! I've got to go!"

A click signified the end of the conversation.

"Me!" exclaimed Snider. "He described me! Me exactly!"

"That's the impression I got," Hayes admitted.

"Now I'm an inside man!" roared Snider to the ceiling. "Has everybody gone insane?"

* * *

Parson was at the pool that afternoon, chatting with the guests in the warm sunshine and smiling benignly at a group of small children who were playing in the shallows with a beach ball. Approaching him from the rear, Sidney Weston slipped a homing pin into the tail of his suit jacket, then casually continued on, collecting empty glasses on a bar tray.

As soon as his brother was out of view, Tom strolled nonchalantly onto the scene and smoothly removed the pin from Mr. Parson's coat. At the same moment an overzealous youngster took a tremendous swing at the beach ball, knocking it high into the air away from the pool. It came sailing down right at Tom.

Boom! The homing pin punctured the ball, which exploded in Tom's face. There was a shocked silence, which was broken when all ten children began to cry simultaneously.

Hastily Tom shoved the evidence into the sand of a nearby ashtray as Mr. Parson walked over to him. "Weston, what on earth did you do that for?"

"Well, sir—"

The manager held up his hand. "I don't want to hear it. Your indiscretions are becoming more and more frequent. If you intend to stay here at Pine Grove, this has got to stop. Now find those poor children another beach ball *at once!*"

Tom ran off.

*   *   *

In the main office at Ontario Provincial Police Headquarters a group of young officers was gathered around the water cooler.

"This is the last straw!" said one of them. "The letter that came in today was referred to us from NATO!"

"There ought to be a law against wasting our time like this!" commented another. "Where does this Weston guy get off writing all these lousy letters?"

"I wish he'd commit a crime! Then we could grab him and nail his hide to the wall!"

"The captain says we can't do anything. The letters aren't obscene or threatening; they're just stupid."

"Yeah, but it's nice to think about it," said the first man dreamily. "Sidney Weston—whoever he is—behind bars, far away from pen and paper."

10

A toast to my toilet

Sidney stared at the screen of his homing device. Tom was on morning duty, and Sidney was taking advantage of his brother's absence to check on the location of his four suspects through the transmitting pins he had planted on them.

"What kind of stupid plot are they running?" he wondered aloud to Blackie and Vishnik's dog. "Doesn't anybody move?" The four pins on the scope were absolutely stationary.

Sidney checked the calibration. One pin was on the lawn—Vishnik, probably. There were two around the swimming pool—at this hour of the morning? And the fourth one—Bishop's, obviously—was in the gym.

The machine must be malfunctioning. Sidney took the back off and checked all the connections. Everything seemed to be all right. Why was nobody moving? Sure, people sat down, but not

without moving for half an hour. Certainly not on the lawn, by the pool, in the gym!

Bewildered, he went out to investigate.

*   *   *

Parson hurried to the receiving area in response to an urgent call from the staff there. He arrived in time to see the driver of an Acme Novelty truck unload a seventh and final crate. All were the same size and bore identical markings: *Caution—Fireworks*. Momentarily he met the worried eyes of his head receiving clerk. Then he was distracted by the voice of the man from Acme.

"That's all of them. Don't know what you're going to do with all this. There's enough fire power in these cases to wage war on the free world. Sign here, please."

Parson gaped at the requisition. For some reason he had overlooked this one at his desk: twenty super skyrockets, thirty Roman candles, twenty pinwheels, thirty shower flares, two hundred and fifty hand sparklers. And the signature at the bottom—Walter Parson.

"Uh—yes," stammered the manager. "This is quite in order. You see, we're having a wiener roast."

"Well, let me tell you, you could roast a lot of wieners with this stuff. Mind you don't roast yourselves," the driver chuckled. He got into his truck and drove off.

"You really ordered all this?" asked the clerk incredulously.

"When the Pine Grove Resort has a wiener roast," said Parson stiffly, "we make it a memorable event."

*   *   *

Sidney crouched behind the potted palm outside Parson's office. Vishnik had just stormed in to see the manager, and it was vital to Sidney that he hear what was being said.

"Okay, you! Parson! Time is almost up! Vishnik gave you forty-eight hours! Forty-eight hours is tomorrow morning! You must act tonight!"

A bell rang in Sidney's mind. Tonight—the wiener roast. Could the big party somehow be connected with the move against the air base?

"Now, now," Parson was saying. "Why don't you just relax? I'm sure everything will be fine."

Vishnik pounded the desk. "While you are having wiener roast, important things must be done!"

Sidney's mind worked furiously, correlating the new information with the data he had already collected. Parson and Vishnik were both members of the plot. What else could they be talking about in such threatening tones? It had to be. The move against the air base would be made during the wiener roast.

His thoughts leaped to a new path. If tonight was the big night, what were the other conspirators doing—Waghorn and Bishop? Breathlessly he dashed down the hall to the gymnasium.

Had he stayed an instant longer he would have heard the angry artist cry, "Tonight by midnight you will find Vishnik's dog!"

* * *

Sidney ran towards Lawrence Waghorn's suite as only a detective closing in on his prey could run. He was now more convinced than ever that tonight was the night of the strike against Trillium; Bishop had been undergoing a heavy workout in the gym, preparing, no doubt, for an extremely active night. He would probably provide the muscle for the strike team.

A maid had mentioned that Waghorn was in his room, and Sidney now approached the oak door quietly, pulling a stethoscope out of his pocket. He fitted the ear pieces into his ears and placed the disc soundlessly against the door. He could hear Waghorn, apparently talking on the telephone.

* * *

"Chief, everything's ready ... What do you mean 'hallelujah'? It hasn't taken that long. And I had to have time to make sure everything fit together. Anyway, I'm ready now ... Of course, I'm sure! Everything's perfect ... Look, chief, don't worry. You'll have it after tonight. 'Bye."

Waghorn sank into an easy chair and sighed with relief. The script was done, everything was fine, and he was still as hot a writer as he had

ever been. No longer did he entertain even the slightest regret over not having gone into his father's delicatessen business. The script was finished, and it was one of his best efforts yet. *Spy story: hotel*—what a great idea! And best of all, that low-down Fuller woman had failed in her efforts to pick his brains. His counter-espionage measures had been perfect. Hiding the script in a waterproof bag in the toilet tank was sheer genius. *No one* would ever think of looking there. Fuller would have to go back to her boss and admit defeat.

The work was over. It was now time to relax, have a drink to celebrate, maybe even go to the wiener roast. Sure, why not?

* * *

Well, thought Sidney, this was it. He sat on his bed, absently stroking Blackie and Vishnik's dog. Tonight would be the strike against the air base. There wasn't time to notify the agencies; there was barely time to warn the base. Tonight he was on his own against four master criminals—Vishnik, the mysterious, evil European artist with a fine eye for detail and a terrible temper; Bishop, the dangerous, lithe, athletic henchman; Parson, the autocratic, highly-placed host for the others; and Waghorn, leader of the organization, and perhaps the most dangerous of them all.

Could Sidney Weston, working alone, be a match for this well-oiled espionage machine? The

conspirators were obviously highly experienced. Look how they seemed to have found the homing pins and disposed of them. That was the only explanation of why they were not showing movement.

Sidney gritted his teeth. He was not ready yet, but by midnight he would be ready for anything!

The door opened and Tom stumbled in, exhausted. "Man, this wiener roast is going to kill all of us! I never worked so hard in my life!"

"I'm really busy too," said Sidney. "I've got to go."

"Where are you going?" Tom didn't really care where Sidney was going, or even if he put those little pins on everyone in the county. He was just too tired to follow. "Make sure you get back by one," he went on. "Check the duty roster. We got stuck with taking care of the little kids this afternoon."

It was deliberate, thought Sidney knowingly. Parson must have sensed that he was more than a mere service boy. The manager no doubt wanted to keep him busy so he couldn't throw a monkey wrench into tonight's plans. Now, what could he do when he was stuck with all those kids . . .

*   *   *

Corporal Hayes switched on the tape of his most recent phone conversation with the voice. Captain Snider listened intently.

"Hi. It's me." The voice was a scarcely audible whisper. "Listen carefully. I may not have time to repeat this. Waghorn, Parson, Vishnik and Bishop are—"

An authoritative voice cut in. "You—Tom—off the phone. There's still a lot of work to be done on the wiener roast. Hop to it." The line went dead.

"That's it?" asked Snider.

Hayes nodded. "I checked out everybody named Tom on the hotel staff. There are seven of them."

Snider shook his head. "We'll just have to forget it, Hayes. The test is tomorrow. Just pass the word on to Simcha the next time he calls in."

"But, sir, he never calls in. He hasn't called once yet."

"He still hasn't called? What the devil is he doing there?"

At that particular moment Simcha was at the pool explaining to three bikini-clad sunbathers where he got his military haircut. It seemed he would have to cut his explanation short, however, as he was due on the tennis court in ten minutes.

"Should I have him paged, sir?" asked Hayes.

"No, let him keep his cover. I'm sure he knows what he's doing."

*   *   *

Tom stood in the centre of the children's play area, looking miserably at the forty hyperactive youngsters he was expected to keep busy for the

174

afternoon. They ranged in age from four to ten, and were all so excited about the prospect of the wiener roast that they could scarcely keep still. And, Tom reflected glumly, there was no sign of Sidney.

"Who wants to play soccer?" he called hopefully.

The reply was a chorus of 'not me's,' snorts of disgust, angry sneers and hisses and boos. One little girl cried.

Great, thought Tom. "Who wants to play baseball?"

Same response.

"Who wants to play strategic espionage immobilization?" came a voice from behind Tom. He wheeled to see Sidney running towards them.

There was a loud chorus of cheers. One of the older boys said, "Sure we'll play it! What is it?"

"I'll explain it to you," said Sidney with great enthusiasm. "First we divide into four teams. You ten over there, the other teams beside them." The division took place with the usual amount of bickering, Tom having to break up a few fist-fights. "Good. Now the oldest person on each team is the captain. I've brought everything we need. Tom, hand each captain a coil of rope."

Tom was more than a little confused by this, but he was so grateful to have something for the kids to do that he obeyed without question.

"Okay," Sidney continued, "now we name the teams. Group one, you're Team Vishnik; group two, you're Team Waghorn; group three, you're

Team Parson; and group four, you're Team Bishop."

"Sidney!" cried Tom in protest. "What are you doing?"

Sidney handed each captain a photograph of the team's corresponding suspect. "Okay, each team study its picture thoroughly. That is your man. Now I'll explain the game. This afternoon is just the practice session. We play the real game tonight at the wiener roast."

There was a roar of cheers.

"Sidney, what's going on?" Tom was becoming alarmed.

"What you're going to do tonight is just go there and find your man, but nothing else until I give the signal. Then the object of the game is to be the first team to have its man flat on the ground, tied up."

Tom was horrified. "Sidney!"

The kids were delighted. There were cries of "We'll do it!," "Fantastic!" and "It's about time we had some fun around here!"

"That's for tonight. What are we going to do now?" called someone.

"We have to practise," Sidney replied. "Okay, the secret word is *Shakespeare*. Remember that. Shakespeare."

Tom was curious in spite of himself. "Why Shakespeare?"

Sidney shrugged. "I want to be the only one to say the word, and it's very unlikely that anyone else will mention Shakespeare at a wiener roast." He turned back to the four groups. "Okay, now

Tom is going to help us practise. Tom, go stand by those flowers." Mystified, Tom jogged off. "When I give the word, you pretend Tom is your man. You get him on the ground, then tie him up so he can't move his arms and legs and all of you sit on him. Got it? Good. Team Vishnik—*Shakespeare!*"

The ten boys and girls were onto Tom like a shot. They bowled him over like a freight train and had him tied up and immobilized in seconds.

"Excellent!" approved Sidney. "Okay, untie him. Team Waghorn, get ready. Well, get up, Tom. They have to knock you down, you know."

The practice session went on until four that afternoon. By that time Tom was caked with dirt and thoroughly exhausted.

Sidney called the teams to order. "Okay, everyone, practice was great. Boy, are we ever going to have a good time tonight!" There was enthusiastic cheering. "Don't forget to take a nap so you can stay up late. We need you all at your best out there tonight. Captains, make sure you bring the ropes. And one last thing—this is a very, very secret game. Are we going to tell our parents about it?"

"*No!*" chorused forty voices.

"Good. See you tonight."

* * *

The Pine Grove Resort Hotel was serving a light dinner at five to tide the guests over until the eleven o'clock start of the wiener roast.

Once again things had changed at Table 19.

Lawrence Waghorn had come out of his shell and was now the life of the party. He had ordered champagne for the table, using his large expense account, and was radiating good will to all, even Miss Fuller.

Some were less receptive than others.

"Vishnik doesn't understand what is going on with this stupid table! First she"—he pointed at Fuller—"starts talking about spies all the time! Then he"—indicating Kitzel—"drives everybody crazy with his daughter and his income tax! Then there is big fight. Then he arrives"—pointing at Simcha—"and talks like protocol officer. Then everyone starts talking about stupid wiener roast. And now used-to-be sourpuss"—pointing to Waghorn—"is making with the ha-ha and buying champagne for everybody. And all this time Vishnik's dog is not with Vishnik!"

"Enjoy it, Mr. Vishnik," grinned Waghorn, refilling the artist's glass.

"Bah!"

Cobber reached for his glass. "You want to lay some of that there bubbly on me, mate?"

Richard Knight put an iron grip on Cobber's wrist. "No, no, no." In a voice audible only to his partner, he added. "You don't drink tonight, Cobber. You're driving."

"Aw, Dick—"

"Let's play the spy game," suggested Edna Fuller.

"I'd love to, but the spy game is over," beamed Waghorn. "I won. You lost. Have some more champagne."

"Now that's sensible," approved Mr. Kitzel. "Say, do you think I should bring my tax portfolio to the wiener roast tonight?"

"That's a wonderful idea," snapped Miss Fuller sarcastically. "I hear there's going to be a big bonfire."

Vishnik guffawed, then snarled as Parson approached.

Simcha addressed the manager. "Request permission to bring my ukelele to the wiener roast, *sir!*"

"Permission denied," mumbled Vishnik, Miss Fuller and Mr. Kitzel.

"What a capital idea," said Parson. "You are a remarkable guest, Mr. Simcha. I've never seen such an active person."

"Thank you, *sir!*"

"I don't see why the spy game has to be over," complained Miss Fuller.

"Oh, shut up!" muttered Mr. Kitzel.

"You and your stupid old income tax!" she retorted.

There were moans all around the table.

"Well," said Parson brightly, "as long as you all seem to be—uh—enjoying yourselves, I'll move on." He made a break for Table 20.

"Just one little drink, mate?" Cobber whispered.

"No."

"Have some champagne, Mr. Simcha," invited Waghorn.

"Don't mind if I do, *sir!*"

"Everyone's going to the wiener roast, of

course?" asked Richard Knight conversationally.

"Vishnik will go to wiener roast," snarled the artist, "so on stroke of midnight Vishnik can wring stupid Parson's stupid neck!"

Everyone else was going to the party. At last Table 19 agreed on something.

* * *

"Welcome to Trillium Base, General McAllister." Colonel Cartwright stepped forward and saluted.

General Steven B. McAllister returned the salute and grinned broadly. "Good to be here, Colonel. We're all looking forward to the test." The general turned his glance to Weinberg. "Nice to see you again, Wings. How's it going?"

Weinberg saluted smartly. "Hello, sir."

"And this is Captain Snider," said Cartwright.

The security officer and the Norad general exchanged greetings, and McAllister introduced his staff of five—a colonel, two majors, a captain and a second lieutenant.

"Well," said Colonel Cartwright, "they're holding dinner for us at the Officers' Mess. Shall we go?"

General McAllister nodded. "Fine. But first"— he hesitated—"I have something to ask you."

One of his majors snickered.

"This will probably sound kind of strange, and we realize that it couldn't happen in a million years, but—is there *any* reason at all to believe that someone might perhaps be intending to steal the Osiris?"

180

"At Trillium?" asked Cartwright incredulously. "Never! Trillium is a fortress!"

Captain Snider cleared his throat carefully. "Well, sir, we've had our share of crank calls, but no direct threats. And anyway, intending to steal the Osiris and actually doing it are two different things. Our security is absolutely sound, sir."

General McAllister and the Norad contingent exchanged meaningful glances.

"Okay," the general said at last. "You've taken a load off my mind. It's—just a little something we've got going back at headquarters." He grinned. "I'll tell you about it sometime. Okay, let's go eat."

Captain Snider led the way to the Officers' Mess. Cartwright brought up the rear, weak with relief that Wings Weinberg was once again his old professional self, with all that Cobber nonsense forgotten.

* * *

Tom returned to his room that evening to find Sidney hard at work with his chemistry lab. He glared unkindly at his brother's back and got angry snarls from the two dogs in return.

"What are you doing?" he asked.

"Oh, nothing."

"Now look here, Sidney. I've been following you around for the past ten days and I know you're up to something. I've delivered your mail from the armed forces and NATO and Norad and all those other people, and I saw those pieces of

carbon paper you kept stealing. I've lived in danger of my life with these two dogs in a room where you can't take three steps without running into some hidden piece of equipment. And this afternoon I was the punching bag while you trained a junior Murder Incorporated squad. Sidney, I'd been looking forward to this summer job since Christmas, and you've turned it into a nightmare. So tell me what's going on. You owe me that much."

Sidney leaned back in his chair and regarded his brother. Even though he knew that what he was doing was absolutely necessary, he felt a twinge of guilt about Tom. He'd have to tell Tom something—perhaps a bit of the truth, without really spilling the beans.

"Remember that plot I was telling you about? Well, Waghorn, Bishop, Vishnik and Parson are going to put it into operation tonight at the wiener roast."

Tom sighed heavily. "And what if it happens that they do? What can you do about it? You're only a kid."

"I have to do something! The future of the whole western world is at stake!"

Tom grabbed his brother by the shoulders. "Sidney, it's about time you forgot about the western world and started thinking about yourself! You're losing touch with reality! You have no hard evidence that anything at all is going on!"

"I've phoned the air base and warned them to be on the alert—" Sidney began.

182

"Right," agreed Tom quickly. "Excellent of you. Now you've done your duty and it's up to the rest of the western world to save itself. Well, I'm glad that's settled!"

"But I must have a plan," muttered Sidney, not to Tom but to himself.

"Say, *I've* got a plan," said Tom. "Since the wiener roast is the big cover, why don't you go to it disguised as a service boy? You'll do exactly what the other service boys are doing and no one will know that, in actuality, you're defending the western world."

"But what's the plan?"

"The plan," said Tom coldly, "is to keep our jobs and stay out of jail."

"Tom, you can't take this so lightly!" Sidney slumped down, deep in thought, absently stroking Blackie's ear. The dog opened one eye, growled at Tom and went back to sleep. "I never should have told you these things in the first place."

"What things?" cried Tom. "I already knew all that! If you want to tell me something important, tell me what kind of slop you're cooking up with that chemistry lab."

"It's nothing you'd be interested in."

"Look, if you don't tell me what that stuff is I'm going to bash your chemistry set into slivers!"

Sidney looked at his brother. Tom was dead serious.

"If you must know, I'm mixing up some delayed-action sleeping drops. I got the formula from *Counterespionage Digest*. I'm using the rec-

ipe for five-hour delay. It's almost seven o'clock now. I'll give some to Waghorn and he'll be out right smack in the middle of the wiener roast."

"What? Sidney, you can't just go around drugging people like that! Isn't it enough that you're going to sic those bloodthirsty juvenile delinquents on him?"

"I have to be sure," said Sidney, returning to his work.

"How are you going to get him to take it?" asked Tom. "You can't just walk up to the man and offer him a glass of knock-out drops."

"He's in the bar right now, and I'm due there to clean tables. I'll just slip it into his drink."

"Sidney, I won't allow it! You'll end up in jail!"

Sidney turned momentarily and faced his brother. "Tom, I didn't want to involve you in this, but you insisted on knowing. It's bigger than both of us. There's no going back now."

*   *   *

Richard Knight strolled around behind the hotel, past the laundry and the maintenance area to the Pine Grove dog kennel.

The kennel keeper looked up as he entered. "Can I help you, sir? Do you have a dog here?"

"No, I'm just touring the grounds. I wanted to see the facilities. I might bring my dog along the next time I stay at this hotel."

"Well," said the keeper, "what you see is what

we've got. It's just an ordinary kennel. We feed the dogs once a day and exercise them twice—in the morning and around midnight so as not to disturb the guests."

Knight smiled. He had already noted this schedule. He had also noted that the dogs were fed a dog biscuit before each walk. These treats were kept in a box which sat on the table that the kennel keeper used as a desk. When the man turned away to soothe a restless poodle, Knight deftly pulled a large handful of identical biscuits from his jacket pocket and placed them noiselessly on top of those in the box. The lightning motion was complete long before the kennel keeper turned around again.

"Very adequate facilities. Good evening." Knight strolled out of the kennel.

The biscuits he had added contained a powerful stimulant. There was no way the kennel keeper would be able to control sixteen hyperactive dogs on their midnight walk during a loud party and fireworks display, certainly not with the extra fireworks he planned to add. And especially not since he had all but severed each lead on the master leash, the one the keeper used to walk all the dogs at the same time. It was going to be a lively wiener roast.

*   *   *

Lawrence Waghorn sat at the bar finishing his second drink and glorying over his completed

script. He drank a silent toast to his toilet, where the script was hidden, drained his glass and called for another.

As Waghorn sat with the second drink in front of him, the highly trained eye of Sidney Weston darted from the ashtray he was polishing to the back of Waghorn's bulky wool sweater. Deftly he tossed a homing pin and watched with satisfaction as the pin caught in the knit of the sweater. Good. Waghorn was tagged. That way, after tonight's crime the police would have no trouble tracking him down. Too bad Sidney didn't have time to do the same for the other conspirators.

As he returned to his ashtray polishing, he did not see his brother dash into the lounge, upset Waghorn's glass and brush the homing pin off his sweater to the floor. Without being seen by the bartender, Sidney or Waghorn, Tom fled from the room.

The bartender turned around. "Well, sir, looks like you knocked over your drink."

Waghorn, who had been daydreaming about his script, looked up. "I did?"

"Don't worry. I'll fix you another."

As the bartender was mixing the drink, Waghorn got up and went to buy an expensive cigar—hand-rolled, maybe. Why not? After all, this was a celebration.

With Waghorn gone and a fresh drink standing at his place, Sidney saw his opportunity. He put down his cloth and began to walk purposefully towards the bar. He whipped out his trusty eye-

dropper, emptied its contents into the drink and left the lounge.

Bert Cobber jogged nervously up to the bar. No sign of Dick, he noted, eyes darting about. Dick would kill him if he saw him in here. He would never understand. It was nothing serious— just a little case of nerves. One drink would take the edge off nicely.

Not that there was anything to worry about, Cobber told himself. He was a great pilot. Of course he could fly the Osiris—no sweat. But he did wish he'd spent a little more time studying the flight manual. Not that he wasn't ready. No way! And— Hey, what was that? A free drink!

It was an omen, Cobber decided. Fate wanted him to have that drink so his nerves would be settled for the big flight tonight. He reached out, took Waghorn's drink and downed it in one gulp.

"Ah! That was good!" See? His nerves were better already. Still, he'd better get out of here in case Dick came along looking for him. Cobber headed purposefully for the door. Nestled in the heel of his shoe was the tiny homing pin Tom had brushed from Waghorn's sweater.

Waghorn returned, puffing triumphantly on a large Havana, saw the empty glass and ordered another drink.

* * *

Lieutenant-Colonel John Daniel "Wings" Weinberg closed the flight manual for the Osiris HE2.

He knew it all inside out. Anything else in the manual would be the words he himself would add after the test flight.

He lay back on his bed. If that plane flew in practice the way it did on paper it would be the most exhilarating experience of his career. He had a really good feeling about tomorrow, except... the image of a fleeing car, the driver turning back and grinning... of a leering face at his bedroom window... The army said Cobber was dead. What if the army was wrong?

Wings turned his mind to the challenge that lay ahead, but he could not shake the nagging feeling that Bert Cobber might appear out of the woodwork at any moment.

*　　*　　*

At Ontario Provincial Police Headquarters the usual water-cooler crowd had one topic of conversation.

"I hate that guy Weston!" muttered one officer. "He just keeps writing and writing!"

"Yeah," agreed another. "I asked the captain if we could bust him on a public nuisance charge. No chance. He's not annoying the public; he's just annoying us."

"Hey," called an officer from his desk, "I think I've got something."

"Don't bother us, Harry. We're trying to think of a way to get rid of Sidney Weston."

"No, listen. You know this Pine Grove Hotel business with the stolen dogs report?"

"So what?"

"Look," Harry persisted. "I've got one of Weston's letters here. It's from the Pine Grove Resort. And in it he says that he kidnapped a couple of dogs!"

There was a stunned silence.

"Here. Read it."

The first officer ran over and grabbed the letter. He threw back his head and roared with joy. "Harry, I love you! I'm going to take this in to the captain!"

He disappeared into the inner office and emerged a few minutes later, grinning from ear to ear. "I don't believe it!" he announced. "We've got Weston! Come on, Harry. The two of us'll go and bring him in. It's a long drive, so we'll have to leave right away. As it is, we won't get there until after midnight." He sighed. "We're finally going to nail Sidney Weston!"

There was a big cheer.

11

Shakespeare!?

Sidney glanced at his watch. Ten minutes past
ten. The staff was supposed to gather for the
wiener roast at ten-thirty. He looked over at his
brother sprawled on the bed. I'll let him sleep for
a while, Sidney decided. I'm sure nobody will notice if he's a bit late. Silently he let himself out of
the room, careful not to wake his sleeping twin or
the two slumbering dogs.

There was vigorous activity going on at the
first tee of the golf course. The kitchen staff was
busy setting up food tables, and several service
boys were piling up wood and kindling for the
huge bonfire. Other service boys were carrying big
boxes and bags of supplies, and some were setting
up a large platform that would be the stage for
the Uptown Schoolhouse Jazz Band. The band
itself had arrived, and the musicians were carrying instruments and sound equipment over to the
site. Out in a sand trap three hundred metres
down the fairway, two firemen were setting up
the fireworks display.

A lot of the guests were already there, especially the ones with small children who were excited and not willing to wait until eleven o'clock. Sidney noted that Parson and Bishop were on hand, but Waghorn and Vishnik were not. He saw Mr. Parson looking at him and immediately went to help some other service boys. He must act as if nothing were going on. It would not do to have Parson suspect that he knew tonight was the big night.

*   *   *

Walter Parson surveyed his first-ever wiener roast. What a wonderful idea of his this had been! Every single guest was present—nearly five hundred people. Everyone was eating and drinking and talking and dancing. The music was a trifle loud and brassy, but the guests seemed to like it and that was the main thing. Listen to the laughter! It was like New Year's Eve with party hats, noisemakers and balloons. The fireworks at midnight would be the crowning touch. What an evening's entertainment! He was a genius!

"I don't care about your stupid income tax!" Miss Fuller informed Mr. Kitzel. "If I've told you once, I've told you a hundred times, I don't care about you, or Sarah, or her expensive education!"

"Just look at how much tax I paid in 1967," insisted Mr. Kitzel, holding out a neatly typed white form.

Lawrence Waghorn finished his hot dog and accepted another mug of beer, reflecting that per-

haps he was a little tipsy and didn't need any more. Oh, what the heck! Who was counting anyway? He popped a charred marshmallow into his mouth, gave a loud blast on his noisemaker and took a long drink. As he tipped his head his party hat fell off.

Vishnik sat cross-legged on the grass, the reflection of the fire on his face giving him a satanic appearance. He checked his digital watch. *11:22*. It would soon be midnight, and there was no sign of Vishnik's dog. He would take this stupid hotel apart and stuff it down Parson's throat. And he would find Vishnik's dog.

Dave Bishop stood by the fire, deftly roasting three hot dogs with each hand. "Here, kids, here's your wienies. Now go and watch the band or get some balloons or something."

"Oh, no," said the taller boy, the one with the coil of rope over his shoulder. "We like to watch you."

"Well, you're getting too close to the fire," said Bishop.

The youngsters stepped back but did not go away.

Lieutenant Simcha was having a glorious evening. He was dressed in gleaming white tennis shorts and a loud Hawaiian shirt with palm trees on it. The shirt was open at the neck to reveal several stylish chains and easily the best suntan in all of Pine Grove. He was draped in pink streamers, with several helium balloons tied to each wrist. He wore two party hats, and his noise-

maker never left his mouth. His ukelele was lying on the bandstand.

He was dancing up a storm with one of his many admirers. "I love the way you dance, Mr. Simcha," she gushed.

"Thank you, *ma'am!*" he responded, careful not to lose his noisemaker. "If I may say so, *ma'am,* you're rather good at it yourself."

Bert Cobber was hovering around the beer table. He was hoping to shake Dick so that he could have a beer—just one—because his nerves had started acting up again. Tentatively, he reached for a bottle. The iron grip he felt on his shoulder signified that he had been found. He was marched away from the refreshment area.

"Aw, Dick, I'm thirsty!"

"There is plenty of lemonade," said Knight icily, indicating another table.

"C'mon, Dick, just one!"

"No."

"Why not?"

Knight sighed. "Cobber, tomorrow morning you will have enough money to buy yourself a brewery. After tonight you can drink as much as you like. You can rot your liver into pulp for all I care. But tonight you belong to me, and you will do as I say."

"All right, mate. You're the boss."

Sidney was patrolling the wiener roast, watching for anything that was suspicious. He noted with satisfaction that his youthful attack teams seemed to be in position; several of the kids had

already approached him to declare their impatience to begin the game. They would have to wait a bit longer, though, as things appeared rather ordinary at the moment. Waghorn and Vishnik were just sitting on the grass, Parson was mingling as he always did, and Bishop was helping out with the cooking.

Things were quiet now, Sidney reflected, but that was probably deceiving. He didn't trust the self-satisfied smile on Waghorn's face or the demonic expression displayed by Vishnik.

Parson watched the noisy revelry with great joy. Oh, yes, his wiener roast was definitely a success. He would ask for a raise after this.

*　　*　　*

"What's going on over there?" Captain Snider asked one of the sentries outside the Officers' Quarters building. "Is the hotel on fire or something?"

"No, sir. It seems to be a big party of some kind. The sentries on the perimeter phoned in and said you ought to be notified because they're so close to our fence. It's quite a row. They've got a band and a big bonfire and everything. And there are hundreds of people, all of them with noisemakers and balloons and stuff."

"They're sure making enough noise," said Snider. "They woke me up."

Colonel Cartwright appeared in the doorway.

"What's that racket?" He spied the bonfire. "What's going on?"

"Big party at the hotel, Colonel," Snider replied. "They sure are whooping it up."

"They've got a lot of nerve blasting out the whole countryside like that! And the night before *my* test!" exclaimed the commanding officer. "Listen to that awful music!"

"What's going on out there?" came the voice of Wings Weinberg.

"Go back to bed, Wings. You need your sleep," advised Cartwright.

"No problem, Colonel. It gets the adrenalin running. Besides, who could sleep with that going on anyway?"

"I agree," said Cartwright in annoyance. "They shouldn't be allowed to make so much noise at this hour. It's half-past eleven! They're disturbing my whole base! And tonight of all nights!"

Snider looked around. It was true. Men, both on and off duty, were standing singly and in groups watching the big wiener roast and listening to the swelling noise. There were lights on in both the officers' and the enlisted men's quarters.

General McAllister wandered out of the building, followed by two members of his staff. "What is it, Cartwright? Are you having a party and you didn't invite me?"

"Private party, sir," replied Cartwright. "A big one. I'm afraid there's nothing we can do about it except try to get some sleep."

"Looks like a good one," said McAllister wist-

fully. "I suppose it's off-limits to servicemen—even generals."

Snider grinned appreciatively.

"Well, let's all go to bed," said Cartwright.

General McAllister sat down on the stairs. "I'll stay out a bit longer. I'm not very tired."

There was general agreement.

"Weinberg needs his sleep tonight," protested Cartwright.

The Norad general laughed. "Wings can fly better in his sleep than most people can awake. Besides, there's such a thing as too much sleep. Wouldn't want to be groggy tomorrow."

Wings grinned and sat down beside McAllister.

"I guess I'll stay out too," said Snider. "If my men see me, they'll pay more attention to duty and less to that party."

"Oh, all right," muttered Cartwright. "We'll all stay out."

From the wiener roast, the sound of hundreds of voices singing "Down by the Old Mill Stream" wafted over the air base fence. They were led by a dominant, braying male voice.

"My God, would you listen to that!" exclaimed McAllister. "It sounds as if they're torturing somebody over there!"

*   *   *

The band was taking a break, and super-guest Simcha was up at the microphone leading the entire party in some rousing choruses of "Down by the Old Mill Stream."

"Couldn't I have a beer, Dick? Just one?" asked Bert Cobber. "Look at that Larry Waghorn guy. He must have had five or six already."

"Yes, and he's flying without an airplane. There's no time, Cobber. We're leaving now."

"For real?"

Knight nodded. "For real. It's twenty-five minutes to twelve." He stared at the long feather Cobber now held in his hand. "Put that rubbish down and follow me—quietly."

"But, Dick, I have to take this along! It's my lucky feather! I wouldn't fly without it!"

Wordlessly Knight reached out, snatched the enormous peacock feather and broke the shaft in ten places. "It wasn't lucky for the feather. Let's go."

"*Dick!*"

"Pipe down. We're leaving."

Knight led Cobber along the fence, away from the glow of the bonfire, a hundred metres past the sand pit where the firemen were waiting for the fireworks display. The two spies, dressed entirely in dark clothing, melted into the shadows as they moved rapidly to the spot where Knight had made the gate in the fence. Silently they disappeared into the bushes.

* * *

Tom was having a dream about bells—church bells, wedding bells, sleigh bells, bicycle bells, school bells, door bells, alarm bells— Alarm bells?

He sat bolt-upright in his bed. The room was

resounding with a loud clanging sound. Was the building on fire? No, the sound was coming from inside the room.

Over the noise he heard growling and whining. He looked down to see Blackie and Vishnik's dog, angry as usual, irritated further by the unexplained ringing. All at once Blackie leaped up at him. Tom dodged and jumped off the bed. Vishnik's dog lunged too, but Tom managed to sidestep him. Then the two dogs, barking wildly, cornered him against the wall by the bureau. Baring their teeth, they moved closer and closer.

Desperately Tom leaped up onto the bureau, his knee knocking against the television set and sending it flying. It crashed heavily to the floor right in front of the two dogs. They yelped, and both ran under Sidney's bed. The bell noise was even louder now.

Oh, no, thought Tom, Parson will kill me! Hey, what was that? He reached down under where the TV set had been and pulled up Sidney's eighty-dollar purchase. He stared at it in amazement. This was the source of the loud bells. But why? What did it do? There was a large rotating disc on top, and a strange screen with dots and lines on it. Tom examined the screen. There were small labels—*front lawn, hotel building, back lawn, swimming pool, air base fence*—and small green dots scattered around the screen. Tom stared. One dot, just inside the air base fence, was pulsating green and red with the sound of the bell.

It all hit Tom with crushing force. A homing device! Sidney was keeping track of his suspects on this thing! Those pins! They must have been homing transmitters! Sidney must have placed some that Tom hadn't got rid of! And now at the wiener roast— The wiener roast? Oh, no, it was 11:45! As if everything else weren't insane enough, he was late for the wiener roast!

Tom watched the screen, transfixed. The flashing dot was moving in a smooth arc further and further onto air base property. His heart missed a beat. One of Sidney's suspects had broken into the air base!

It was unbelievable! Sidney had been right all along! Tom wondered who it was—Waghorn, Vishnik, Bishop or Parson. Another thought occurred to him. Sidney couldn't see the screen! He would not know that the operation had already started!

Tom stood up on the bureau, fists clenched. *It was up to him, Tom Weston, to save the western world!* He leaped down, flung open the door and dashed out.

Two heads poked out from under the bed. Tom was gone. Both dogs flew out the open door on the dead run, away from the bells.

* * *

"Dick, what did you do to the guards?" whispered Cobber in horror in the darkness of Hangar B.

"Nothing permanent. They will simply have

recurring headaches for a while. All right, Cobber. Get into the cockpit."

"Without a pressure suit? In the Osiris? Are you crazy?"

"If you follow my instructions, you won't need a pressure suit," said Knight. "You'll be flying relatively slowly and low. You do remember the plan?"

Cobber yawned. "Yeah, yeah, mate, okay. Should I leave immediately?"

"Not yet. Now listen carefully. Get in, switch on your radio and wait until you hear from me. I have a transmitter that is on your frequency. When I give the word, you press this remote control button"—he put a small switch-box into Cobber's hand—"which will open the hangar door. Then you taxi out to the runway as quickly as possible and take off."

"Got it, mate." Cobber climbed into the cockpit, gave Knight a thumbs-up sign and yawned again.

Knight turned to leave. "Make sure you stay awake," he warned.

Cobber laughed. "Who could fall asleep in a spot like this?"

Knight climbed back out the window and was gone.

What a guy! thought Cobber admiringly. He looked at the gleaming control panel and was relieved to find that he recognized it from the sketches in the manual.

He reclined in his seat and yawned hugely.

Why was he so sleepy? He wasn't really tired, and he ought to be wide awake from tension alone. He picked up the switch-box Knight had given him and examined it. It looked more like a toy than anything else—or a disconnected door-bell.

Cobber felt his eyes closing and snapped them open resolutely. If he fell asleep and goofed this up... He felt himself slipping again and started slapping himself vigorously in the face.

The closer the time drew to the five hours of Sidney's delayed-action sleep drug, the more trouble Cobber had staying awake. The remote switch dropped from his fingers and bounced under the seat. His head nodded. At three minutes to midnight Cobber was fast asleep.

*   *   *

The Pine Grove kennel keeper fed the last fox terrier his dog biscuit, hooked his sixteen charges up to the large master leash and opened the gate. He was, he reflected, the most unfortunate person on the staff. Absolutely everyone was at that wiener roast; that is, everyone except him. He had to stay with the dogs because Parson was afraid of another theft. Too bad somebody didn't steal Parson. Now he was the only one missing the food, entertainment and free beer.

He noticed as he walked that the dogs were a little skittish, probably because of the big bonfire

and all the uproar. Maybe he shouldn't have taken them out tonight.

The noise of the wiener roast covered the sound of two loping shadows approaching from behind. As twin barks erupted from Blackie and Vishnik's dog, the whole band of dogs wheeled, barking in reply. The wrench on the master leash pulled the keeper to the ground.

From behind the clump of bushes where he had set up operations, Richard Knight's keen night-sight picked up the churning mass of dogs. He had been expecting it. His watch read one minute to twelve. Without hesitation he pushed down the small plunger on his control mechanism.

There was a loud explosion, and ten metres of the air base fence rose into the air in a huge fireball and disintegrated. There were screams from the wiener roast.

All sixteen hyperactive dogs broke their weakened leashes and trampled their keeper as they sped, howling and yapping towards the explosion. Blackie and Vishnik's dog were hot on their heels.

On the front steps of the Officers' Quarters, Captain Snider leaped to his feet and began running madly towards the site of the explosion and the breach in the fence. The other officers followed, and sentries converged from all over the base.

"Cobber, take off!" commanded Knight into his transmitter.

A snore came in reply.

The wiener roast was in a panic. Almost five hundred people began to run away from the ex-

plosion at the fence, towards the hotel. Then, spying the onrushing wave of dogs, they turned around and ran back, bumping into each other. Sheer pandemonium reigned. When the excited dogs caught up and started scattering amongst the people, chaos spilled over through the breach in the fence onto air base property.

"Cobber, take off! Cobber—Cobber! *Wake up, Cobber!*"

"Lemme sleep just five more minutes . . . "

"Hey," said one fireman to another in their pit, "I guess that's the signal to start the fireworks. It's midnight." They shot the first big rocket up into the air.

From the direction of the hotel came a red streak, the figure of Tom Weston running at top speed. All fears cast aside, he ran courageously into the boiling sea of dogs and people, darted through the crowd, leaped up onto the bandstand, grabbed the microphone, inflated his lungs and bellowed, "*SHAKESPEARE!*"

Sidney stared at his brother. "Shakespeare?"

Sidney's highly-trained assault teams instantly forgot the excitement of the moment and launched themselves like bloodhounds at Waghorn, Parson, Vishnik and Bishop. In a matter of seconds the four bewildered suspects lay on the ground, trussed like turkeys.

The first rocket exploded in midair.

"*Cobber!*"

"Huh?"

"Wake up, you fool!"

Captain Snider was shouting to his men. "Bust

up that riot! Those civilians are going to get hurt!"

"What's going on?" asked Wings Weinberg.

"Shut up and keep running!" snapped Cartwright.

"Cobber, you will wake up *this instant!*"

In the cockpit of the Osiris HE2 Bert Cobber was drifting between semi-consciousness and awareness. He could hear Dick's voice. Dick seemed angry and— Oh, no! Now he remembered! He was in the Osiris! He had fallen asleep! He felt himself drifting away again ...

"Take off, Cobber! *Take off!*"

"Yeah, yeah, mate, I'm going," Cobber mumbled. With shaking hands he started the engine. The sparks were brighter than the bonfire as the hyper-ellipsoid nose cone of the Osiris HE2 tore through the still-unopened hangar door and headed for the runway.

"The Osiris!" chorused Snider, Cartwright and McAllister. The air base personnel stopped in their tracks and gaped in horror as the gleaming aircraft took a strange zig-zag run down the airstrip and lifted with a roar into the air.

Knight watched from his hiding place as the Osiris made an unusually sharp bank and began diving for the ground.

"Cobber, *what's going on?*"

Cobber's head jerked back into awareness. He was in the air! A large Roman candle popped only a metre away from the cockpit.

"Dick, they're shooting at me!"

"Pull up, Cobber, *up!*"

The Osiris wheeled and climbed again with a great roar of its engines, and began making perilous zig-zag manoeuvres as Cobber fought against Sidney's sleep drug.

"General McAllister," shouted Wings, "let me go up there in a fighter! I can force him down!"

McAllister grabbed Weinberg by the arm and began to run him towards the hangars. "Great idea! Come on, Wings! We've got to stop him before he gets away with the Osiris!"

Snider and a group of men followed on the dead run.

"Get the jeeps! We'll go back out there in the jeeps!"

The group left Cartwright in the middle of the field, shaking his fist at the sky and shouting, "Come back here with my Osiris!"

"Cobber," ordered Knight, "get away from here!"

Overhead, Cobber was circling erratically among the helium balloons, skyrockets and Roman candles, desperately trying to stay awake.

Flat on his back under ten children, all Mr. Parson could see was the exploding sky. "Get off me!" he ordered. "Let me go!"

"No way, man!" said a six-year-old girl. "I think we won!"

Bishop was in a similar position. Even his athletic struggles were no match for the ten members of Team Bishop—they too were claiming victory.

Waghorn did not offer any resistance. He simply looked at his ten captors and said, "Somebody want to go get me another beer?"

The large golden retriever smelled his master in the depths of a pile of youngsters and pushed his nose in to lick the artist's face. There was a hoarse cry of recognition. *"Vishnik's dog is once again with Vishnik! Here is Vishnik's dog!"*

Tom took stock of the four figures on the ground. If they were all here, *who* was at the air base?

Mr. Kitzel was struggling with a large fox terrier which had clamped its teeth on his 1978 tax return.

"Cobber, follow the plan!" ordered Knight.

"I'm having trouble staying awake, Dick!"

"Cobber!"

Edna Fuller, dazed by the enormous riot, accidentally stumbled into Knight's clump of bushes. "You! Mr. Knight! You're the spy, aren't you?"

He looked at her harshly. "My dear Miss Fuller, while you are standing here accusing me, you are allowing Mr. Kitzel to get away scot-free. I hereby deputize you. Kitzel is your man. Go get him."

Miss Fuller darted urgently out of the bushes, dashed into the surging crowd and found Mr. Kitzel. She wrenched his briefcase from his hands and, with all her might, brought it down on the top of his bald head. Mr. Kitzel crumpled to the ground unconscious.

Wings scrambled into a fighter and began to manipulate the controls. General McAllister slammed the door. "Force the Osiris down, Wings! That's an order!"

Wings saluted and fired the engines as Snider and McAllister ran out the open hangar door to the waiting jeeps.

"Cobber, get hold of yourself!" Out of the corner of his eye Knight spotted the take-off of a fighter craft in a smooth, graceful arc. The fighter began to head for the Osiris.

"Cobber, get away!"

"I'm sorry, Dick. I'm really sorry."

"If you don't get away you will be a good deal sorrier," threatened Knight.

Suddenly he heard another voice on his transmitter, the voice of the fighter pilot. "Attention, Osiris HE2. This is Fighter K17. I am armed and have you in my sights. You will land at once or I will destroy you!"

Cobber's voice was sleepy. "Huh?"

"Don't listen to him!" urged Knight. "They would never destroy the Osiris! Now fly it out of here! The plan!"

"Who's that?" cried Snider. "Identify yourself!"

Knight ignored the order. "Fly, you fool! You have more speed! Get that thing out of here!"

"Don't listen to him!" McAllister cut in. "Lieutenant-Colonel Weinberg has orders to fire on you. You'll never get away!"

Surprise momentarily edged the sleepiness out of Cobber's voice. "Wings? Is that you, Wings?"

"Cobber?" Wings' voice barely whispered.

"Yeah, mate! It's me, Bert Cobber!"

"Oh, no!" muttered Snider.

There was a long silence, then the shaky voice of Wings Weinberg: "Request permission to return to base."

"Permission denied!" snapped McAllister. "We've got him over a barrel! Now move in and force him down!"

It occurred to Knight immediately that Weinberg was, for some reason, afraid of Cobber. "Bert Cobber is a very dangerous man," he broke in. "Weinberg, you don't have a chance."

"I know," quavered Wings.

Cartwright's voice cut into the frequency. "What's going on up there, Weinberg? Why aren't you forcing him down?"

"It's Bert Cobber!" Wings' voice sounded preoccupied. "I'm in the same sky as Bert Cobber!"

"Impossible!" cried Cartwright. "Bert Cobber's dead! H.Q. says so!"

"I'm awake!" Cobber's voice returned to the air. "What's going on?"

"Hang in there, Cobber," commanded Knight. "Weinberg knows he's doomed if he tries to tangle with you."

The radio clearly carried Wings' terrified gulp.

On the ground the riot was in full swing. People were still milling around in confusion, the dogs darting among them as the kennel keeper tried to gather them together. Air base people mingled with the Pine Grove crowd, trying to calm everyone down. A forces doctor was at-

tempting to revive Mr. Kitzel. Jeeps were moving madly around the fields, trying to predict the manoeuvers of the two planes overhead, one flying erratically, the second matching its moves exactly but keeping a distance.

Sidney, having checked his captives, was watching the drama in the sky.

"Who is this guy Bert Cobber anyway?" raged McAllister into the radio.

"The most ruthless man ever to step into the cockpit of an airplane," came Knight's voice dramatically.

"Yeah," agreed Wings from the fighter.

"It sounds as if he's asleep!" cried Snider. "Force him down!"

"But—"

"All right, Wings, this is it!" bellowed McAllister. "Get a grip on yourself! You're a Lieutenant-Colonel—*I'm a general!* This is a direct order! If you don't follow it, I will personally court-martial you! Got that! Now, force him down!"

Sidney watched in admiration as the second plane broke out of pattern, arced gracefully and swooped down upon the Osiris. Steadily, with relentless accuracy, Wings angled the fighter's nose down over the Osiris' cockpit, breathing a silent prayer that Cobber would have enough brains to take it down.

The planes were less than five metres apart when Cobber finally came awake enough to take

stock of the situation. Quickly he manipulated the controls and began to descend, swiftly and smoothly.

"Way to go, Wings!" cheered Snider into the radio.

"Keep at him, Wings. Doing fine," came Mc-Allister's voice.

Cartwright covered up the mouthpiece to his radio and marvelled, "What a pilot!"

Richard Knight stared at the sky for an instant, then swiftly packed up his transmitter and disappeared into the shadows. The operation was over.

The riot was beginning to clear up as well. The air base sentries and some helpful guests had finally been successful in calming people down. The dogs were under control, the fireworks display was over, and the bonfire had burned down. Most of the guests were seated around the stage, a safe distance from any remaining activity, listening to Lieutenant Simcha on the ukelele. Simcha, who had convinced himself that there was no way in the world those planes could possibly have anything to do with him, had decided that everyone had gone long enough without some entertainment.

Suddenly Snider's jeep roared through the hole in the fence and screeched to a halt in front of the bandstand. The captain stared in amazement.

"Simcha, what the hell are you doing?"

Simcha interrupted his song and snapped to

attention, rapping his ukelele against his knee and racking his brain for a reply. Finally, he said, "I don't know, *sir!*"

Snider's jeep roared away.

The jeeps were now converging on the hotel lawn, trying to predict the spot where the Osiris would touch down. All heads were turned towards the sky.

General McAllister was standing up in his jeep, and when his driver screeched to a sudden halt, he almost fell over. "What's going on, Corporal? Keep moving!"

"Sir, there are people on the ground! Tied up!"

McAllister leaped out of the jeep and stared. The kids had all been gathered up by their parents, and four lone figures lay tied up on the grass.

"Who are you?" asked McAllister of the man they had almost run down, as he and the driver released the ropes.

The man sat up and embraced a large dog. "I am Vishnik and this is Vishnik's dog."

McAllister's jaw dropped. "You're kidding!"

Vishnik smiled. "You have heard of maybe me?"

"I—I think so." The general pointed to another bound figure. "Who's that?"

Vishnik snarled. "That is idiot Parson."

"Parson," repeated McAllister absently. "And him?"

"Waghorn."

"Uh-huh. And the fourth man?"

Vishnik looked at the athletic director. "He is—um—"

"Bishop?" prompted McAllister.

"Right. Bishop."

"You mean this is the Pine Grove Resort Hotel?" asked the general weakly.

"Yes. A stupid place."

The Osiris forgotten, McAllister jumped onto the hood of the jeep and bellowed, "*Sidney! Where are you, Sidney? It's me—Steve!*"

From amidst a crowd of air base personnel, Sidney wheeled. "Steve? Steve! Over here!"

The Norad general and the Pine Grove service boy ran towards each other and met in a joyful embrace.

"Sidney, I never thought I'd actually get to meet you!"

"I knew you'd come when you got my letters!"

They were interrupted by Colonel Cartwright's half-crazed voice. "He's coming in too steep! He's going to crash! *My Osiris!*"

All watched intently as the Osiris screamed towards the ground, bounced heavily on its wheels and came to a sudden stop alarmingly close to the hotel building. The nose cone, jarred loose by the shock, bounced twice along the ground and crashed through a first-floor window.

Lawrence Waghorn, lying on the ground waiting for someone to untie him, stared at the path of the wayward nose cone. "That's my room," he shouted, struggling to his feet. "Oh, no! The script!" He began hopping furiously towards his shattered window, howling, "My *toilet!*"

Wings Weinberg's fighter circled over the crash site. His shaky voice came over the radio: "Request permission to go back to bed."

"Permission granted," laughed McAllister into his transmitter. He still had one arm around Sidney.

Sidney was saying, "Nobody would have believed me. Even my own brother insisted there was no concrete evidence that anything was going on." He looked around suddenly. "Tom. I wonder where Tom is?"

* * *

"Sir, honestly, I'm not Sidney Weston. I'm Tom Weston."

The officers standing around the small detention cell that held Tom simply laughed.

"Oh, sure," said one of them. "Then how come when we asked people where Sidney Weston was they all pointed at you?"

"Because Sidney and I are twins," Tom explained miserably.

"Don't give us that. There's no way out of it, Weston. We've got you for stealing dogs. It's a shame we couldn't get you for writing letters, but the important thing is that we've got you. And we're going to see to it that they put you away for a long long time."

Tom sat back on his uncomfortable cot. "I really am Tom Weston."

The first man took Harry aside. "Hey, do you

think we could have the wrong kid?" he whispered.

"I don't know," Harry replied. "All those people seemed sure he was Sidney Weston. He comes from the right place—"

"Yeah, but all his identification says Tom Weston."

"He could really be Tom Weston and use the name Sidney just for writing his letters."

"Harry, I think we arrested the wrong kid."

"How could we have? You heard him try to explain what was going on up there—all that garbage about the fate of the western world! That's straight out of his letters! This is Sidney Weston, all right."

"Still, Harry, I'm pretty worried about this. False arrest, you know."

"Well, we can't do anything until the captain gets in tomorrow. He'll straighten it out."

Tom Weston lay down on his cot and tried to go to sleep. He could not take his mind off the hotel and the homing pin that had gone over the fence. It had been up to him. Had he blown it? And Sidney. Was Sidney all right?

12

Our man Weston

The Osiris HE2, its nose cone reattached, its dents and scratches touched up, flew graceful arcs, sharp corners, steep climbs and a whole series of pre-planned delicate manoeuvers, some at low altitudes, and some high up above the clouds.

Sidney Weston sat at General McAllister's side in the control tower, flushed with admiration for Wings Weinberg. General McAllister had secured the day off for Sidney, and he had gone back to the air base with the Norad people. They had swapped stories for the remaining hours of the night, slept for a while during the morning and got up for the big test, at which Sidney was an honoured guest.

For almost an hour the legendary Wings Weinberg had been electrifying the observers and earning praises like "flawless" and "amazing" from those monitoring the instruments. There were loud cheers from the entire base as the Osiris glided in majestically for a perfect landing. Wings

hoisted himself out of the cockpit and leaped triumphantly down the stairs into the arms of his joyous crew.

Sidney smiled broadly. "That was the most incredible flying I've ever seen."

The general nodded. "Wings has really outdone himself this time." He slapped Sidney on the shoulder. "Come on. We're meeting Wings at the Officers' Club as soon as he gets out of his gear. We've ordered a vat of champagne. Surely you can drink a little toast if a general authorizes it."

"What about that man you arrested, that Bert Cobber?" asked Sidney.

"He'll be taken away for questioning to see who hired him," said McAllister. "One way or another, he'll be spending a lot of years behind bars."

"At the hotel he seemed to be with a man named Knight," offered Sidney.

"Knight, eh? We'll check that out. Probably not a real name, though. And I'll bet he's far away by now. Anyway, let's get going down to the club."

There was quite a celebration going on at the Officers' Club. The general's party joined right in, and soon The Legend himself arrived, a little tired but smiling. After all, Bert Cobber would never bother him again. The champagne was poured, and flashbulbs went off to record the historic occasion.

216

General McAllister hauled Captain Snider and his camera over to a quiet corner. "Here. Get a picture of me with Sidney Weston."

Naturally all the other members of the Norad contingent wanted their pictures taken with Sidney too. They finally settled on one shot with McAllister, him being a general, and one group shot with Sidney as the focal point.

"These'll hang on the office wall next to your map," McAllister said, "right over the Sidney Weston filing cabinet. The staff back at the office will turn green with envy when they hear we've met Sidney Weston!"

Corporal Hayes snapped to attention before McAllister. "General, sir, there are two OPP officers at the gate asking to see Sidney Weston. And —sir—the sentry at the gate says they've got Sidney Weston with them!"

McAllister looked at Sidney and grinned. "What else have you been up to? Okay, Corporal, send them in."

"Wings," Colonel Cartwright was saying, "I'm sorry for all the things I thought about you. For a while there I was sure you were cracking up. But you were great in the air today, and you were great last night. Thanks to you, the Trillium-Osiris project was a success. Let's drink a toast together."

He raised his champagne glass and Weinberg touched it with his. The test pilot grinned. "I hope you get a new staff car soon."

"Coming next week," smiled the C.O. "I'll get Snider to walk it home."

"Lieutenant Simcha," said Captain Snider, "what were you doing all that time over at the hotel?"

Simcha thought hard. "I was carrying out my mission, *sir!*"

"More specifically, Lieutenant."

"I don't remember, *sir!*"

Snider grinned. "I thought you wouldn't. I had a talk with Mr. Parson, and your talents as a guest came into the conversation. He was about to present you with his 'Model Guest of the Year' award. I persuaded him not to. And, oh yes, your hotel bill and the fees for various private sports and dancing lessons, and the bar bill for all those lovely ladies you treated, will be deducted from your pay." His brows clouded. "Is that clear?"

"Perfectly clear, *sir!*" He seemed to be in trouble.

"Good. As of now, you are the officer in charge of the Trillium sanitation squad. Do you think you can apply your bronzed carcass to that?"

"I'll do my best, *sir!*"

"I want you to do more than your best!" snapped Snider. "I want you to do your work! That's all."

Simcha saluted. He was not quite sure what had happened to him, but it didn't seem to be very good. He walked out the door just as Hayes was bringing in the two OPP officers who were escorting Tom Weston.

McAllister wheeled and stared at Tom. "Sidney, that explains it! There's two of you!"

"Hi, Tom," said Sidney.

"Is that him?" asked one of the policemen.

"Yeah, that's my brother Sidney."

The two officers started towards Sidney.

General McAllister interposed himself protectively. "What's the meaning of this?"

"We have a warrant for the arrest of Sidney Weston for the theft of two dogs."

"The dogs are back with their owners," said McAllister. "Arrest Sidney Weston? That's the most ridiculous thing I ever heard in my life!" He draped an arm around Sidney's shoulders. "This is our man Weston you're talking about. He's been operating on secret Norad business. I'm General McAllister. I'll take the responsibility."

"You're kidding!" blurted Tom. "You're General McAllister? You're Steve?"

"And you must be Tom," smiled the general, "our other man Weston." He shook Tom's hand. "I've heard a lot about you."

The policemen looked at one another.

"Hey, Harry, I guess we'd better leave it. The guy's a general!"

"Yeah."

The two made an unceremonious exit.

"Well?" said Tom impatiently. "What happened? Did we win? Was the move against the air base stopped? Is the western world okay?"

"Everything's all right," said Sidney.

Tom sighed. "When I found your homing device—"

"Homing device!" chortled McAllister.

"When the alarm went off and I saw the blip go over the air base fence, I just ran like anything and yelled 'Shakespeare.'"

"Shakespeare?" repeated McAllister. "No, no, don't explain it to me. I wouldn't understand it anyway. I'm only a general." He walked off.

"Well, Sidney," said Tom, "I guess we've lost our jobs for sure, eh?"

"I didn't," said Sidney. "You did, though."

"What?"

"Don't worry," soothed Sidney. "Steve persuaded Mr. Parson to keep us both on, and Norad will pay for the broken TV set. Old Parson was so overjoyed at getting his dog back that he was easy to convince—especially when the word came from a general. Besides, he doesn't have the time to fire us. He's too busy mediating the truce between Miss Fuller and Mr. Kitzel. Mr. Kitzel's promised not to press assault charges, and Miss Fuller's promised to give a good report to the income tax people. Everything is fine."

In the midst of the party, Sidney and Tom ran into the immortal Wings Weinberg.

"This is Wings Weinberg," said Sidney in awe. "He's the greatest test pilot in the world." Tom and Wings shook hands. "Hey, Tom, you don't even know who it was who tried to steal the plane. The pilot was that man Cobber and—"

Wings held a finger to his lips for silence.

"Shhh. That's ancient history. From now on we don't mention that name."

Tom looked at his brother questioningly.

Sidney shrugged. "He's not your ordinary test pilot, but he's the best!"

*　*　*

"Guard him carefully," Captain Snider instructed the military police sergeant who was handcuffing Cobber to the seat of the jeep that was to take him away for questioning.

"Yes, sir." The sergeant saluted, got in and drove off with his prisoner.

"Guess I'm going to be going to jail for a long time, eh mate?" asked Cobber sadly as the jeep drove out through the gates of Trillium Base.

There was no reply.

"Eh, mate?" Cobber looked at the sergeant and saw only his own reflection in the mirror sunglasses beneath the MP hat. He sat back in his seat and sighed mournfully. "My mother had plans for me. She wanted me to be a dentist. I wish I'd listened to her. By now I'd have a nice little practice set up, a cozy little house, a wife, a couple of kids . . . "

"Stop snivelling, Cobber."

"Dick?"

Knight took off his sunglasses.

"Dick! It's you! I'm not going to go to jail! You saved me!"

"Don't rub it in, Cobber," said Knight coldly.

"If I had my way they'd lock you up and throw away the key. But if I allowed them to hold you they would undoubtedly question you. And considering your lack of intestinal fortitude, not to mention brains, I felt that some description of me might come up."

"They already asked me about a man named Knight," said Cobber. "Of course I said I'd never heard of you, but I don't think they believed me."

"It is not my real name, naturally," replied Knight, "and I recommend that you change yours as well. More specifically, you are now Howard Banner." He reached into his inside pocket and handed Cobber a thick envelope. "Your birth certificate, driver's licence, social insurance card and passport are in here. Also a plane ticket to Libya—one way. I selected Libya because it is the farthest place on earth from where I will next be. From there you can do what you will." He indicated a bundle on the back seat. "I have provided some clothing. It will fit, of course. In the breast pocket of the suit jacket you will find one thousand American dollars—considerably less than what you would have received had you been successful, but enough to keep you alive for a short period of time. And infinitely more than you deserve."

They entered the limits of a town.

"You are a very lucky man, Cobber. Many with more competence than you have have met with great misfortune as the result of failing me. You are undoubtedly the stupidest person alive; be grateful that you are."

222

He pulled up to a bus station and released Cobber from his handcuffs. "Goodbye, Mr. Banner."

"Gee, Dick," said Cobber, "does this mean we won't be seeing each other any more?"

Knight sighed. "With any luck, yes, that's what it means."

"It sure was great working with you, Dick. You're a real pro."

"Thank you, Mr. Banner."

"I really don't understand what happened to me in the Osiris, Dick. I don't know why I fouled up."

"You will have time on your hands to think about that in Libya."

"Anyway," said Cobber, "I'm really sorry."

"One more thing." Knight reached down, removed the small pin from the heel of Cobber's shoe and tossed it down a nearby sewer.

"Gee, Dick, how'd you see that?"

"It's my business. Good luck, Mr. Banner. You will certainly need it."

Richard Knight drove off. Eleven kilometres down the road he turned the jeep off into the woods and drove through the brush and trees to a spot where a brown Buick was parked at the edge of a cliff. He got out of the jeep and pushed it over the cliff into the gorge below. Then he got into the Buick, returned to the highway and drove away.

Bert Cobber stood in the bus station parking lot, staring down the empty road where Knight had disappeared. Richard Knight was a good spy,

but he sure wasn't very smart! Libya, hmmph! He would cash in the ticket and go somewhere where he could have a good time! Las Vegas! Sure, why not? He had a thousand dollars. He could run that up into a fortune in no time. Grinning broadly, he grasped the envelope and began to walk towards the bus terminal.

*   *   *

"If you'll just calm down for a second, chief," Lawrence Waghorn shouted into the telephone, "I'll explain to you why you can't have the script today! Stop yelling!"

Though it was mid-afternoon, Waghorn had just awakened and was not quite recovered from the horrible events of the previous night. His head ached abominably, and his whole body was bruised and stiff.

"Okay, now, this is what happened. The airplane crash-landed outside my hotel room and the nose cone bashed through my window and smashed my toilet . . . No, I'm not giving you the outline for a new sitcom! I'm telling you the truth! It really happened . . . Yes, an airplane. A big one . . . Right, it crash-landed and the nose cone came off . . . Uh-huh. It came bouncing through my room and crashed into my toilet . . . What do you mean 'what does that have to do with the script?' The script was in the toilet! . . . Because that Fuller woman was trying to steal it, so I kept it in a waterproof bag in the toilet tank.

Then this nose cone thing shattered the toilet into a billion pieces and the script got all mangled and totally water-logged ... Yes, that's it ... Chief, I am *not* lying! It was finished! Really it was! ... Chief ... Chief?"

Waghorn hung up with a sigh, walked across his new room, sat down at the typewriter and began typing: *Spy story—hotel* ...

About the Author

Born in 1963, Gordon Korman began his professional writing career when he was only thirteen years old! His first book, *This Can't Be Happening at Macdonald Hall!,* grew out of a Grade Seven writing assignment.

By the time he graduated from high school, Gordon had written five other books—all of them Canadian bestsellers—as well as articles for several newspapers.

Raised in Toronto and Montreal, Gordon is now studying film and screenwriting at New York University. Current plans include the publication of his books in the United States and a TV series based on his "Bruno and Boots" characters. But even with his busy schedule, Gordon still finds time to lecture and tour extensively in Canada.

If you liked *Our Man Weston,* you can read these other books by Gordon Korman.

This Can't Be Happening at Macdonald Hall!

Boarding school isn't so bad after all! Roommates Bruno and Boots are having a great time making midnight raids on the refrigerator, playing practical jokes on people and keeping their stern Headmaster on his toes. But when they go too far, Mr. Sturgeon decides that the two "troublemakers" have to be separated.

Bruno is supposed to share a room with Elmer Drimsdale, a genius who uses his bathtub for biology experiments. And Boots gets stuck with George Wexford-Smyth III, the school snob.

Naturally Bruno and Boots will do anything to get back to their old room together. And that means Mr. Sturgeon's troubles are just beginning...

Go Jump in the Pool!

"Those turkeys sure can swim." Boots has just lost another swimming race against York Academy. But how can Macdonald Hall ever expect to win a trophy if its team doesn't have a pool to practise in?

Bruno has the answer: raise $25,000 to build one! With the help of the girls at Miss Scrimmage's Finishing School for Young Ladies, the boys organize rummage sales, talent shows and contests. But they can't even begin to pay for a pool, and Mr. Sturgeon forbids them to try any more crazy schemes.

Enter George Wexford-Smyth III with the craziest scheme yet. And if Bruno and Boots can get away with it, they'll make more than enough money for their pool!

Beware The Fish!

If Bruno and Boots don't do something drastic, Macdonald Hall could go bankrupt. Luckily, doing something drastic is what Bruno and Boots are best at. And in their usual considerate way, they won't bother Headmaster Sturgeon with the details.

Using Elmer Drimsdale's electronic wizardry, they launch a publicity campaign to save the school. What they don't know is that the RCMP suspects them of being enemy spies! And with Mr. Sturgeon, Miss Scrimmage *and* the RCMP hot on their trail, it looks as if Bruno and Boots have finally met their match . . .

The War with Mr. Wizzle
(coming in fall, 1982)

Bruno and Boots face their biggest challenge yet. Walter C. Wizzle and his computer, the 515, have taken over Macdonald Hall in an effort to "modernize" the school! But Mr. Wizzle's ideas of modernization include a dress code, demerit points, detentions and worse.

Across the road at Miss Scrimmage's Finishing School for Young Ladies, Cathy and Diane are facing their own crisis. Miss Peabody, a former drill sergeant for the U.S. Marines, is trying to whip the girls into shape.

Could this be the end of Macdonald Hall?

I Want to Go Home!

Rudy Miller hates camp. He hates the smiling counsellors, the happy campers, the organized activities—and most of all he hates being treated like a kid!

When his parents send him to Camp Algonkian Island, Rudy decides to make life so miserable for everybody else there that they'll be glad to get rid of him. The only problem is that all his plans are backfiring, and it looks as if he'll be stuck at camp for a whole summer.

Who Is Bugs Potter?

Dave "Bugs" Potter is in Toronto for the High School Band Festival when he decides to help out a local rock group. The audience loves him and Bugs becomes an overnight sensation, but he refuses to reveal his true identity to his fans.

At the same time, film star Bibi Lanay is in town to promote her new movie—and Bugs is stealing all her publicity! Not only that, someone is trying to steal her most fabulous jewel, the Falusi Emerald. And worst of all, the only person who can stop the thieves is none other than Bibi's arch-rival—Bugs Potter!

Ⓒ

WOM⬛995

~~lience~~
licence of 2 cute guys
a ~~to~~ beige coloured car

"Highwayman Inn & Resturaunt"
Highwayman (the book, the girl's
father was an innkeeper)